MY LIFE TAKE TWO

PAUL MANY

Walker & Company
New York

First published in the United States of America in 2000 by
Walker Publishing Company, Inc.

Published simultaneously in Canada by Fitzhenry and Whiteside,
Markham, Ontario L3R 4T8

Line of poem quoted on page 169 is from e. e. cummings. Firmage, George, J. ed. *e. e. cummings, Complete Poems.* New York: Liveright, 1991: page 511. The line appears in "as freedom is a breakfastfood." (sic)

Library of Congress Cataloging-in-Publication Data

Many, Paul.
My life, take two / Paul Many.
p. cm.
Summary: During the summer before his senior year, Neal, to prove he can be responsible, tries to figure out a way to keep from losing the memories of his dead father while completing a documentary film for class and deciding what he wants to do with his life.
ISBN 0-8027-8708-8
[1. Self-perception—Fiction. 2. Fathers and sons—Fiction. 3. Motion pictures—Production and direction—Fiction.]
I. Title.

PZ7.M3212 My 2000
[Fic]—dc21 99-055396

Book design by Mspaceny / Maura Fadden Rosenthal

Printed in the United States of America

2 4 6 8 10 9 7 5 3 1

MY LIFE, TAKE TWO

ALSO BY PAUL MANY

These Are the Rules

To my wife, Linda,
my mom, Julia, and
the memory of my dad, Paul

"In memory is the more reality."

—Henry David Thoreau

Journal entry, 12/30/1841

Thanks to my editors,
Soyung Pak and Emily Easton,
at Walker & Company,
for helping me to realize this book
and to my wife, Linda Dove,
for some important insights
along the way to writing it.

MY LIFE, TAKE TWO

1

ONE

"THE DOGS ARE almost on us.

"They aren't supposed to be set loose till after dark, but here they are, tearing through the woods, sounding like a baseball clipping through the top of a tree. My dad, who a second ago was showing me some clouds, suddenly shouts: 'Run, Neal! Go!' and here he grabs my arm and it's like when I was playing with that old lamp wire and I get JUMPED into that first step and I'm off the trail and into the woods without thinking—or maybe like a rabbit hearing a rifle shot."

I *knew* this would grab them. Even that frypuppy Nowack quits making fart noises with his hands and looks up. I kick up the light on the overhead so they can see my drawings better.

"AND MY DAD is running, dragging me along. I've never seen him run and it seems strange, like seeing a teacher in his bathrobe getting the newspaper off the sidewalk in the morning. Here you can see my reaction in close-up. And he's making a snorting noise and I look up and he's laughing for cramping up guts! That's how full of life he is; that freakin' everything is funny. It's like we're about to become one of the major dog food groups and all he can do is laugh. And it makes me laugh too, so I have to shout: 'Dad! Stop it!' 'Cause it's cutting my wind.

"In the next few panels here, you see how we come to a high stickerbush hedge and he half throws me over and dives through himself. The dogs are digging and yipping as they try to push through and then leaping so their snapping, snarling heads pop up and down like dumb, dopey puppets, but next they run off.

"Close-up on Dad saying: 'They're going around.'

"Now the thing is, these stickerbushes? They're supposed to keep people from falling into the Chasm. . . . Wait, here's the close-up . . . this giant gouge in the earth that's maybe a quarter mile long and fifty feet down? And now we're on this narrow path trapped between the dogs and the Chasm. So in this overhead crane shot, you see how we start running on the path, but suddenly, the dogs come around the end of the hedges and 'Whoa' says my dad and here we flip directions.

"We run back, but by then, another of the dogs—you see him in this extreme close-up—the biggest and most vicious spit-spraying mongrel of them all—shows around the other end and I start to climb back over the hedge, but Dad says 'No! This way,' and he grabs my hand and totally trusting, I follow him, stepping out over the edge.

"Cut to camera two. Long shot.

"Now here we switch views and you're looking up from deep down inside the Chasm and you know with that sick feeling in your gut that nobody can possibly stand, sit, or lay down on this—well you can see it's a cliff—but here they are, anyway, these two little specks who fly out over the edge into space, their tiny arms spinning like helicopter blades, trying to stay up as they run down the crumbly dirt and sand, except each step they take is two feet out and eight feet down, so it's like they're taking giant steps or skiing without skis or snow, or brains.

"You see them going faster and faster with these huge Godzilla steps and there's no way they can keep up straight and keep on running, but somehow they do it for two or three more and—right when it looks like they're going to wipe out—here in this panel you see the man SPROUTS A PAIR OF GOLDEN WINGS! And here, we cut to this medium shot, of a woman up on the edge shouting at the dogs, holding them back, as if they'd be stupid enough to do what these guys just did.

"Here in these next ones, you see it from her point of view: the

magical wings unfolding from the man like he was a human Swiss Army knife, how he scoops the boy up in his arms and they spiral down, down, down lower and lower, finally landing with a couple of big steps like from skydiving, in the dry wash at the bottom.

"Then the big shimmery wings fold back in and, in this last panel, the two go off whistling like what just happened was just another ordinary thing on another ordinary day.

"Fade to black and The End," I say to the class, killing the light on the overhead.

Everybody sits quiet in the dim room.

Finally, I hear Mr. Bhandaru's voice from the gloom somewhere in back: "Very nice, Mr. Thackeray," he says. "You draw well. But you are supposed to be making a documentary in this class, not a cartoon."

"But Mr. B," I say, "I swear, that's what happened."

"Remember," he says, shooting up the shade so everybody jumps. The sun blinds me for a moment.

"Sometimes reality can lie."

2

Ever since I took Mr. Bhandaru's Documentary Filmmaking class last term, it's been bothering me just how bizarre my memories are. I found I've got these pictures in my head that are perfectly logical in every possible way, except for one: they make no sense.

It first hit me when he had us do this presentation to the class where we had to storyboard some experience in our lives—you know, where you draw cartoon panels of the scenes? And it was only when I started to draw where my dad sprouted the wings that this struck me as being totally weird.

Oh yeah, I'd *thought* about it before, but it was one of those things you never really *think* about, like why Monday is called Monday or howscome most of the continents are wide at the top and pointy at the bottom or like that.

By now I've learned to deal with *personally* losing it, but when these twisted memories start causing me *reality* problems I really start getting edgy.

Case in point: We're supposed to make this documentary for the class? Well, this storyboard was my last, best shot but because it's so strange, Mr. B kills it.

The unfair part is that Mr. Bhandaru himself has "Strange" listed on his teaching certificate under "Specialty Area." Item: He goes by the stage name "Movie Maniac" on his weekly, late-night movie show of the same name on local TV. On the show he wears a cape and, from experience in a past life that happened totally in his mind, talks like he went to Famous Actors' School.

So when he tells me my idea—which I spent the whole last two weeks drawing—isn't acceptable, while I'm still lying there in a pool of my own flop drool, he hits me with this:

"The key to making a good documentary is to be *generous* with your images. But you are like a tiny little child who hides behind his hands and imagines the space there to be his own tiny little world. Except it is the *camera* you are hiding behind instead! You hold on to it. You hold back. You must learn to get out from behind it and *reveal* yourself if you are to make pictures you *really care about.*"

And even though he's such a wacko, this last part really got to me. Since my mom yanked us from the estate back when I was a kid—like ten years old—and then my father died only a couple of months later, my life has all the excitement of a dud fireworks show:

WHOOOOOOSH!

(pip)

Yay.

There just wasn't *anything* that really got to me anymore. So I do what I do best in this kind of situation: Give up and wallow in defeat.

In the end, The B-man probably felt sorry for me. Instead of the F that I hoped he'd give me, so I could be through with it, he gives me an incomplete and says I can have the summer to work on my movie.

My girlfriend, Emily, by the way, sees my mixed-up memories as only one more act in my one-man reality-juggling show. She knows me better probably than anyone on the planet. You see, before we were even born, her parents and mine were friends, and from the moment we clawed our way out of the birth canal together on the same day in the same hospital (different mothers), they probably planned it that we'd get married.

"Your problem, you poor, poor Neal," she once told me, "is that you get the real stuff mixed up with all the other stuff." She says this so sweetly and sincerely that I truly appreciate her for telling it to me straight, although lately, I'm getting more and more the feeling that she does it out of frustration.

And I do so *desperately* need Emily to help me keep fan-

8

tasy and reality separate especially since the few memories I have of my dad are all I have left of him and if I start getting them wrong—if I somehow start screwing *them* up—he'll be gone for good.

Anyway this is getting way ahead. So let me start here:

It's the last week or so of school and I'm sitting in French class chewing over the news from Mr. B about the incomplete and trying to figure how I'm going to get it done before next fall when I'm supposed to be a senior. I'm ignoring the PA—which is basically one of those fast-food drive-up speakers anyway?—when, right after the lunchroom menu (Hawaiian Sloppy Joes and lime Jell-O with pineapple), it cuts out and comes on again with:

"Sqawwwwwwwweeeeene wantsa sum ajob, hum a tomato afta skoo."

"You want fries with that?" I say to the guy next to me, and we both laugh—in French of course ("Ew, Ew, Ew, Wha-ha").

It was only later, when I ran into Emily's mom, in between classes in the hall, that I realized I'd let something else slip by.

"So you're going down and apply?" she said.

"For what?" I said.

"Didn't you hear on the PA? 'Anyone wanting a summer job should report to the office after school.' " Mrs. J was the school secretary and purse-bumping buddies with my mom and they had this regular conspiracy thing trying to find some use for me.

But even if I did understand the PA, I probably would have ignored it anyway. Like I said before, Why bother?

"Why not?" said Emily when I mentioned the possibility to her later in the cafeteria.

"Well, maybe you forgot," I said. "I was so good at jobs last summer, I got fired from two of them."

"Three, wasn't it?" Emily always brought lunch from her home planet where tofu was the staff of life. She had some slabs of the slimy brown stuff mixed with lumps of orange stuff in a plastic container.

"Right," I said. I wasn't up for luau chow—although the serving wenches looked *so* attractive in their plastic Hawaiian leis—so I was eating a vending machine sandwich that tasted like they forgot to unwrap the cheese.

"Well, just look at it as experience," she said. "You learn something with each job."

"Yeah and here's what I learned: Item A: People blame the paperboy if they sleep late and their sprinklers get their newspaper all wet. Roman numeral two: If their French bread is covered with shampoo when they get home, it's the bagboy who did it, and Rule C: They blame the busboy for not being a mind reader when they go to the bathroom and they aren't *completely* finished with their tapioca. I mean, where is people's sense of personal responsibility these days, anyways?"

Emily rolled her eyes like she did every time I went on one of my rants. She poured some juice with ploppy bits of stuff in it into a plastic cup.

"There's always the money, Neal," she said.

"We're doing OK," I said.

Even though Dad didn't believe in insurance, Mom had taken out a policy that paid off our debts; we had a couple of cars that ran and Mom had gone back to work after Dad's heart attack, anyway, so that usually made up the difference.

"What is it anyway, this job?" she said, waving around an orange lump on the end of her fork.

"I don't know," I said. "I have to go down to the office and find out. What do you think? Should I try again?"

"See what it is and if it seems OK, go for it. Neal, I think you're making too much of this."

"Remember what I told you my dad used to say about 'the next logical thing'?"

Of course she did, I'd only told her about a thousand times.

"It's always the next logical thing, Neal-o," my dad always said. "You're born a slick slimy little grub, they blot you down and stick a hat on your head, then as soon as you can eat solid food and keep from pooping your drawers, it's off to school and college and a job. You get married, have a bunch of kids and buy a house and a station wagon with drainpipes. If you don't keep your eyes open, you find yourself waking up one day and asking, 'What the heck am I doing *here?' "*

"Of course I remember," said Emily. "You've only told me about a thousand times."

"Well it always makes me think twice."

"Thinking isn't bad," she said. "But then you've got to

do something." She snapped the lid on her plastic container, screwed the top on her juice bottle, and packed it all away in her backpack.

"Look," she said, "I've got a meeting after school today and a big accounting test tomorrow, but at least go down to the office and check it out. Then we can meet tomorrow and you can tell me all about it."

"OK," I said.

"The usual place?" she said, giving me the Significant Look before she turned and left the cafeteria.

3

THREE

"Just a minute. Just a minute, I *know* I saw it," says Mr. Reynolds, the assistant principal, before I can even open my mouth.

The second he sees me through the little window in his office door, he's scowling, piling up big thunderclouds of crabbiness, probably thinking it's more of the usual.

So while I stand there, he keeps pawing through the mound of red trouble slips like he's a dog digging for a mole. Finally he sighs. "I give up. What is it *this* time, Thackeray?"

"The job," I say.

"Oh yes, the job, job, job. . . ." he says, renewed in his paper smooshing. "You mean from yesterday?"

"Yup," I say.

He suddenly stops.

"It's *you* that's applying?"

13

"Well, I was kind of thinking . . ."

"It's for a relative of mine, you know," says Mr. Reynolds. "I'm doing this as a *favor* for him."

I thought I knew what he was driving at. And I had to agree with him. I'd been working hard to live up to what some of the guys had been calling me since the time with the water balloon in the auditorium: "CB"—short for "Crash and Burn."

"I'm sure I can handle it, Mr. Reynolds," I say anyway. I put my hand on the back of my neck, which is suddenly feeling ticklish.

"Ah, here we go." He pulls out a piece of paper and holds it up by two fingers like it was the rotten fish someone (I swear it wasn't me) stuck in the toilet tank in the teachers' bathroom. It's torn and has what looks like a tire track across it. Through the dirt and stains I read:

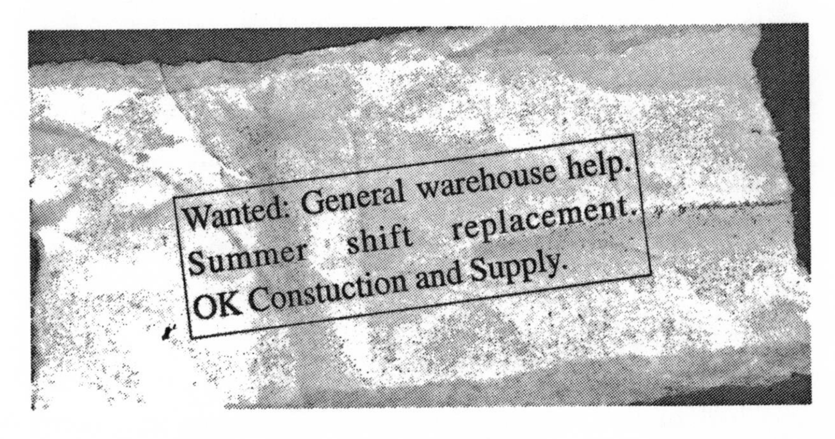

Wanted: General warehouse help.
Summer shift replacement.
OK Constuction and Supply.

"Con-*stuck*-tion?" I say, holding my nose so it sounds like I have serious booger backup.

"Let me see that," says Mr. Reynolds, snatching it from my fingers.

"Construction," he says. "It's supposed to be Con-*struc*-tion."

"Lots of people ask about this?" I say, a small glimmer of hope sparkling behind my eyeballs.

"A couple, but no takers," says Mr. Reynolds. "But don't get your hopes up."

I promise him that I won't and he holds it out for me to take. But when I try to, he won't let it go, until finally a corner rips off.

I should have been suspicious.

No takers?

And let's not even *talk* about the spelling for a minute, but who would go and name a business "OK"?

I mean, would you fly on "All Right Airlines," get your teeth pulled at "Could Be Worse Family Dentists" or—I hate to even *think* about it—get an operation at "Not So Bad Brain Surgery"? ("Hey, don't be so picky. Most people don't use more than ten percent of their brains anyway. Am I right? Blink if you can hear me.")

But I went down there after school, anyway—some squat gray building near the railroad tracks with a raggy American flag drooping from a rusted pole.

The lady at the desk said the secretary was out sick and she had to find the applications. I filled them out pretty quick, since I didn't have too much to admit to in the "employment history" part.

Then I sat for a long time reading a magazine called *Preformed Concrete Monthly,* which was kind of like *Playboy* for cinder blocks. Finally she showed me to the gray, steel desk of Mr. Spiro, this grouchy-looking, bald-headed guy in a white short-sleeved shirt and clip-on bow tie, who smelled like that fishy smell in the dry cleaners?

He was reading my application and he twitched his head at me like he was going into a spasm. I guessed that meant I was supposed to sit in the chair next to the desk, so I did. Every once in a while he squinted and took quick, jerky hits from a can of soda, sometimes dribbling some on the desk where he kept a paper towel to soak it up.

I felt nervous, like I was waiting to get back a term paper where I'd made up a few quotes, since I'd stretched the dates a little on all my hit-and-run jobs to make it look like they fit over the whole summer. So to take my mind off things, I started carefully looking around—a habit my dad taught me.

On a calendar hanging behind Spiro, some babe in a bathing suit held out a pillow with a golden rivet lying on it like it was the Rare Diamond of Pittsburgh. A row of giant books with pieces of paper sticking out of them was lined up underneath. On top of his file cabinets and computer were all these little figures—a girl on a bicycle, a kid on a swing, a guy pressing a barbell, and maybe twenty others—all made out of stuck-together nuts and bolts.

Outside his office door, real people, chilled by the fluorescent lights, were running around with their fists full of slips of paper, or were sitting, zonked, in front of computer screens. Farther on I could see out into the warehouse, where gray droogs were pushing carts around in the dimness.

After a minute, with my stomach gurgling like a coffee-maker since I didn't have anything to eat since lunch, Spiro spoke:

"Reynolds sent you?" he said, without looking up.

"He told me about the job," I said, which wasn't the same thing, of course, but Spiro didn't seem to notice. Instead he sighed and looked me in the face.

"Mr. Thackeray, is this *all* of your experience?"

"All?" I wanted to say, If you had wanted *all* my experience, I would have written down everything my dad taught me about how to really *see,* or shown you the drawings I made on the estate of the May apples that grew around the Big Tree, or the exclamation points of tadpoles in Strider Pond. I would have brought in the fat photo album full of my sketches of the deer that came to drink there in the morning, or the ones showing the steep, black lines of trees against the snow in the open fields along Snake Creek. Or I'd have lugged in the storyboards for my documentary, which you'd better snap up now before Hollywood gets a look at it.

But instead I said, "Yep, that's all of it."

He frowned but then seemed to shake it off. Then asked

Did I drive?

Yes.

Did I use drugs?

Aspirin.

Could I start the following week?

School would be over, so what could I say, but "Yes"? He made a note or two, took another swig of soda, and stared level in my eyes long enough that I looked away.

"We've got some big projects coming up," he said. "I hope you're not one of those guys who's afraid of a little hard work."

I said I wasn't, and was going to add But I still check under my bed for it every night, just to make sure. I figured he wouldn't get it, though. Then he stood up and grabbed my hand with one of his and my elbow with the other, as if he was going to put me in a hammerlock.

"We'll let you know," he said, and used the hold to shove me out the door.

It wasn't until I was nearly home that I realized I didn't even ask what they paid.

"Well, how did it go?" said my mom as soon as she walked in the door that night. I didn't even ask how she knew. I'm sure Emily's mom had filled her in on everything.

"I don't know," I said. "They said they'd call."

"As in 'Don't call us?' " she said, still wearing her Death of a Saleswoman suit as she flipped through the mail on the kitchen table. She worked some dumb job downtown where people called up and yelled at her all day, and it usually took her a little while to cool off.

"They didn't say that," I said, trying to pretend I was truly interested in when exactly the spaghetti water was going to boil.

"Well, what *did* they say?" she said, trying to pretend *she* was truly interested in the fifty-percent-off coupon from the Cheese of the Month club.

"Not much, really."

"Did it look like the kind of place you'd want to work in?" she said.

"Mom," I said, "I don't know. I don't know about it at all."

She dropped the mail on the table, and stood next to me at the stove.

Unlucky for me, even if I agreed with my father that work was a wet brown bag full of green meat, my mom had other ideas. She thought that it built character and self-reliance, would give me good posture, neat grooming habits, help in the shrinking of warts, and keep my coat shiny. But once, completely frazzled when I blew my third summer job last year, she let the true reason slip: "Neal," she said, "you've got to get on with your life."

"I know it's been tough for you, Neal," she said, "but you can't just be sitting around all summer."

"Mom," I said. "What do you think I'm doing? If this doesn't work out I'll try something else."

She put her hand on my cheek like when I was ten and fell off my bike. I shook her off.

"Look," she said. "I guess I just don't know how to talk to you anymore."

She stood there for a few seconds as if she was waiting for me to come back at her, but I said nothing.

I wanted to say it was Dad who used to do all the talking

anyway and might still be doing it if *she* hadn't insisted that he quit the caretaker's job and that we leave the estate.

She started to lean over to kiss me on the forehead.

"Mom," I said, ducking her, "the water's boiling."

Wouldn't you know it was just my luck?

Next day they called and said the job was mine.

4

IN THIS FIRST panel—a long shot from across the street—you see me walking in front of a huge, graffiti-decorated warehouse wall, under a big red OK Construction and Supply Co. sign and into a dark employees' entrance.

Next there's a couple of close-ups:

A hand pulling a time card with my name on it out of its slot.

The time clock, which reads exactly 8 A.M., ker-chunking as the card is pushed into it.

In a medium shot, Mr. Spiro steps out of his office and motions me to come with him.

Then you see a bald-headed guy wearing triple-thick eyeglasses and gray coveralls, standing at a counter. He's got a pencil behind

21

each ear, and is nervously eating peanuts from a brown grocery bag as Spiro and I come into the frame.

"This is Lou," says Spiro, "He'll be your supervisor."

"I just quit smoking," says Lou, looking down.

There's an insert of an ashtray mounded high with broken peanut shells.

In the next medium shot, Lou reaches under the counter and takes out a bucket and a scrub brush, which he hands to me.

"Come with me," he says.

Then we're back across the street in a long shot again where you see me and Lou walk out the employees' entrance.

"There you go," Lou tells me, nodding at the graffiti-covered wall.

"What?" I say.

"Get to work," he says. "Scrub off as much as comes off," and he turns and leaves.

In this last panel, you see me sigh, dunk the brush in the bucket, and begin scrubbing.

This is, of course, my first few hours at OK Construction—storyboard style.

With Bhandaru on the brain, it's like I've started storyboarding my whole life away—experience, memories, dreams—you name it. Maybe it's not the best way to get a grip on things, but it helps to pass the time.

22

The wall was so full of drawings and other stuff, it looked like a block-long comic book. The mighty midgets who went to the school around the corner must've gotten their giggles from dragging their crayons around the big blank gray front of the building.

I guess it made me realize how far down I'd sunk when I had to kneel to be low enough to scrub off their misspelled munchkin markings ("Misus Poleta Suks"). I looked around every once in a while, afraid that one of the guys from school would come by and see me.

Funny, but I don't remember ever hearing that those big-time, way-rich, computer geeks started like this. Dunking their sleeves in a bucket of soupy gray water? Getting their chinos all blotchy with soapsuds washing a big, dirty building?

By noon that first day, though, I knew that working at the OK Construction and Supply warehouse would be special. I was just coming into the lunchroom when the long picnic table that the warehouse workers were sitting at collapsed at one end, sending a wall of doughnuts, foam cups, bottles, and paper wrappings surfing down the tabletop on a tidal wave of spilled coffee, and dumping a couple of benchloads of the workers in the middle of this soggy mess.

Stupid me, but up until then, I believed in live and let live. I had the crazy idea (OK, whack me with the goof stick) that people who had to work together would try to get along. But I couldn't have been more wrong.

You see, the workers at OK basically fell into one of two warring armies:

The warehouse guys who picked orders and tracked everything from toilet bowls and two-cent bolts to valves as big as a car and tiny control parts you could fit up your nose if things got dull. These guys suffered from caffeine poisoning, running in all directions filling orders, the forklift with its light spinning and beeper beeping as it zipped through the aisles.

Then there were the guys in the construction crews—carpenters, plumbers, electricians—who were much more laid back, chewing on toothpicks and joking as they got their orders filled in the mornings before wandering out to their trucks and disappearing to Who-Knows-Where for the day.

If the warehouse guys could mess with a faucet so it sprayed a construction guy in the face when he installed it, or fix a hammer so the head flew off, it was high fives and grins for their side.

If a construction crew could unscrew a bathroom doorknob so it trapped a warehouse guy, or, let's say, rig the lunchroom table so it collapsed when the warehouse workers sat down to eat, it was thigh slaps and chuckles for *their* side.

As the new employee who bounced from job to job in the middle of all this, I was like one of those squinty dimwits who's standing around making their Christmas club payment and gets taken hostage in a bank robbery.

And sure enough, next day while I'm pushing a cart stacked high with orders, a wheel comes off and the whole big heap of stuff comes crashing down like a car wreck. In case somebody slept through this, some monster drain cover goes spinning like a giant coin down between the rows of desks in the sales office and falls over.

I see that somebody has pulled the pin that held on one of the cart's wheels—the thing isn't going to fall off all by itself, is it? So I put the wheel back on, stick in a bent nail to hold it, and pick up all the pieces.

"Rough luck, Richie." It's Vinnie, the forklift driver—the same guy who the first day of work tries to sell me a hot TV.

("Still in the box, man," looking both ways as he dragged on a smoke out in the loading bay. "I know someone who got a couple dropped off a truck by mistake. Good deal, man. You should get all over this.")

But I guess when I told him Sorry, I wasn't interested; that I was saving my money for college, it was a double insult. ("You don't smell too bad for a hairy person.")

"OK, Richie, hold onto those lucky bucks, college boy," he said.

Then he starts calling me this—"Richie"—all the time. Like in "Heads up, Richie!" when he nearly runs me down with the forklift.

But, in spite of all this, I vow I'm going to hang on.

Did someone ever tell you to go shove something "where the sun don't shine"? Well, that's where my next assignment was. Maybe I should put it this way: if the OK Construction warehouse needed an enema, this was where they would stick the nozzle.

Mr. Spiro takes me back into this butt-dark pit himself so I can make personal friends with a huge pyramid of boxes piled up to the roof beams about the time of the original Egyptian models.

He tells me to break down and bale up this mountain of soot-covered cardboard and he "doesn't want to find me goofing off back here, since it's not too late to hire somebody else who is willing to do an honest day's work."

By now, believe it or not, I'm actually *ready* for this. It's like the time when Guernsey, the art teacher, didn't even *tell* me about the state art competition. "It was on the PA," he said. Well yeah, but he made a special point of asking a couple of the other guys. I worked day and night and had him enter me anyway with some of my storyboards, which I colored in like newspaper comics? And I didn't go on to state, but I did get like third in the whole district.

So I'm eager to show Spiro I can do a good job. I spend the day cutting and folding and baling so the back of my throat is all black and I'm coughing up an honest day's worth of dirtballs.

Next morning when I punch in there's a note stuck on my time card: "See Mr. Spiro."

I knew it! A primo performance! And now once they see what I really *can* do, it's the executive express escalator for me, a gold-plated whoopee cushion, and free hot wax coupons for the company car.

But instead Spiro looked like someone had mixed some jalapeño powder in his hemorrhoid cream. (Don't look at *me.*)

"Thackeray," he said, sounding strangely like Mr. Reynolds, "You are the one responsible for baling up all the cardboard?"

I said I was, puffing out my chest in case they needed extra room for the medals.

"And you put it out on the loading dock?"

Just so. Neatly stacked against the wall.

"Well, I don't know what kind of idiot would deliberately leave it out there in the rain all night. *You* don't look that stupid to me. But someone needs to get back there and unbale it and spread it out to dry."

Should I have told him that *Vinnie* was the one who told me to leave it there last night so the recyclers could get at it before we opened in the morning? And that afterward I never even gave it a second thought, snug in my feetie jammies at home, sleeping to the pitter-patter of raindrops on the roof above my bunk bed?

"To *dry*?" I said.

"You don't think we're gonna throw it all away after we paid you to salvage it, do you? We can't get anything from the recycler if it's wet, so get out there and get busy." He went to take a swig of his soda, but realized the can was empty and fired it into the wastebasket. "Now!" he added, since I was still standing there with my mouth hanging open.

I'm a little slow, I guess, and it was only then, as I cut the

27

ropes on the bales and started peeling off the soaked cardboard, that I started to feel my neck getting flushed and hot and something working my jaw and curving my mouth into an expression that wasn't a smile. But for the sake of proving that I could take it, I swallowed it all down.

I set the stuff out to dry in the second loading bay—which looked like it wasn't much used judging by the amount of junk heaped next to the door—and also in the large, unpaved side lot where the big rigs came in to wait to be unloaded on busy days.

As I was working, Vinnie showed up in one of the delivery vans, spinning his wheels as he backed it over the cardboard I'd laid out. He had one skinny arm hooked out the window where I could see he had a foggy green tattoo of a dagger with a snake wrapped around it and some blurry words underneath. ("Born Too Loose"?)

"Rain last night, Richie?" he said, leering through the patches of hair pasted to his face that he was passing off as a beard.

"Yeah," I said, feeling like I'd like to spread him out to dry *under* one of the semis.

"Well," he said, trampling over a couple more pieces of cardboard, as he got out of the truck, "looks like you've found your level around here . . . the bottom. Har, har, har." This last wasn't a laugh, but something he always said after something else that was supposed to be funny.

I bit my tongue and turned away, back into the dark of the warehouse.

5

"Well it's a good thing you didn't come back at him, Neal," said Emily when I told her the next afternoon all that happened at work. "Vinnie sounds like a real creep—dangerous even. And if you got in a fight . . . I bet that Spiro guy would've called Reynolds on you."

"Yeah, and they'd take away my sharp crayons, put me in detention until I was thirty, and stamp a big frowny face on my Permanent Record."

Emily had a big puzzly look stamped on her face as she pushed us back and forth on the old, busted lawn glider. It was like I never gave her the kind of answer she was looking for.

But my motto is "When you're doing the wrong thing, do *more* of it." So I tried harder. "Spiro never told me what to *do* with all the cardboard when I had it all bundled. And

I *swear* it was Vinnie that screwed up the wheel on that cart so it would fall off. And I mean breaking up all those old boxes . . . is that all I'm—"

"Neal," she said, stopping me in mid-rant, her fingers cool on my lips. "They're *testing* you, don't you see? They start you out with the *stupid* jobs. They want to see how well you take orders. If you do OK at *those* jobs . . ."

"I know, I know," I said. "They trust you with the better ones."

Emily raised both eyebrows, her mouth unsmiling, studying me close to see if I really got it.

"But it's all part of a plot to beat you down," I blurted out, feeling pushed into a corner, "to make you a good citizen, a fan belt on the engine of life, a fold-down stairway to the attic of death."

"Neal, ever since you took that film class . . ." She finished the sentence by shaking her head.

What I was really trying to tell Emily was that getting a job was part of my own plot to make myself more than *useless.* You see, in the six years since my father died, "useless" happened to be the one-item-or-less, cash-only, express-line summary of my life.

From the time he was laid out on the floor next to the bed, my mother shouting, "Call 911. Call 911"—from that time on I've not been all that useful. My hands shook so much I called 411—information—by mistake. "What city?" the operator kept asking me and I kept telling her where we lived. If I had only thought to run next door to get someone's help or something . . . but even the paramedics said that with such a massive heart attack there wasn't much anybody could do unless it was done right away and with the special equipment and drugs they had. Of course I always wonder if they said that just to make me feel better.

It didn't work.

The one bright spot in all of it was Emily. She had been there through the darkest days after my father died when no one else could or would talk with me and she stayed by me through everything, the best antidote to my misery. Over the years she even tried to pull me out of it. In fact lately she had become stubborn as far as self-improvement was concerned—mine, that is.

As I said, Emily had been nearly promised to me since we were born together. There's even a picture of the two of us next to each other in the same crib in the hospital. Growing up, we played house and doctor. ("Paging Dr. Thackeray. Detailed anatomy exam needed in basement.")

We even had a fake wedding in the sixth grade in social studies and had to take care of a hard-boiled egg for a week. (I left it out on the table at home and our dog ate the whole thing including the shell, so I boiled another one and nobody knew the difference.) And although neither of us had come out and said it, it looked like real marriage was going to happen as soon as we finished college.

Emily-No-Nonsense-Straight-Up-Front-Johnston was a whizzy-wig—a "What You See Is What You Get" kind of person. The package didn't lie, and it was a pretty attractive

31

one. Emily was exactly my height in bare feet and kept her hair short and straight, and her hair is not something I'd even notice, except she dyed it a bright red unlike any found in nature. Her eyes were hazel-colored and looked plain, not like you see in the magazines where sometimes they paint their eyelids green or something, but had their own natural aliveness. Her nose was slightly turned up, and her mouth— Well, her mouth—that was a whole other world. It was wide and inviting and she had a way of biting her bottom lip that made me bite mine.

"Neal, we're going to be seniors in the fall," Emily was saying with that inviting mouth of hers. "We've got to start getting serious."

"But I am getting serious," I said, switching from "we" to "me."

"Yeah, like the thing with the fish?" she said.

"That wasn't me," I said. "I swear it. I know this warehouse job is only a summer thing, but . . ."

"I'm starting to get scared, Neal."

"About the fish?" I thought. Talking with Emily lately was like trying to tune a car radio on a long trip where you didn't know the stations.

"About my job?" I said, when she didn't say anything for a while.

"About everything," she said. "Like we have to start applying for colleges. And for business colleges, you have to apply even earlier." She gave me a sideways look.

I should mention that part of Emily's Program for Me

would be that I would go to college for something useful—like business—which I think she saw as something like army basic training that would knock some responsibility into my thick skull. In spite of what I told Vinnie, though, about "saving for college," I still wondered if maybe I would fit better in a traveling circus.

"I'm going on some campus tours this summer," she said.

"And *that's* what you're scared about?" I said.

"And about us," she said.

Here "we" go again.

"We're doing fine," I said, trying to glide by with a general statement about life.

"But it's like we're stuck," she said. "We need to be going somewhere."

Another sideways glance. Was this an invitation? A promise? A threat? It was hard to tell.

I should explain first of all the kind of thing we were stuck in.

We'd go walking in her neighborhood and from the next block over, through an empty lot, find our way to a storage shed way out in the back of her property—one of those fake barn things where dads keep their lawn tractors, chain saws, and other signs of their fatherly authority? We'd sit on the busted old lawn glider stored there and then . . .

Well, you see, Emily had been helping me cope in at least one other way.

Although in social science class I learned a lot about the

customs and habits of people in other countries, there were people right here in my own neighborhood who I lived with every day and who I knew as much about as:

Pick one of the following:

(a) How to build a nuclear submarine;
(b) The mating rituals of gastropods;
(c) The inside pages of my calculus book;
(d) All of the above.

(Did you choose "d"? You win one of these fine plastic kazoos.)

The several square feet of surface area that every girl carried around on her was virgin territory (in a few cases, anyway) that I knew very little about. It was a region that probably added up to a couple of acres in my school alone and that I was a little late in exploring.

Late, at least, compared to other guys. If you believed *half* of what they said, anyway. (And if you did, I have an A paper on "The Mating Rituals of Gastropods" to sell you.)

And then, three years after my father died, when I turned thirteen, Emily had offered—no, insisted on—serving as my guide through this strange land. For the time I traveled through it with her, for those stolen hours in the lawn shed, I lost myself. Forgot about school and work and my mom and yeah, even my father for a few brief moments.

But in all that time, aside from most things you can do with your clothes on and in spite of my trying to push on, her guided tours had usually stopped at the borders of the deepest unknown regions.

It's not that Emily was cold or anything—she was far from it.

It was only that her practical side included a lot of her outside.

From her business prep courses she had learned that spoken agreements were not worth the paper they're printed on. She needed to see diplomas and certificates before I—or anyone else, I guess—would get to travel any farther.

Unless I could convince her otherwise, that is, and I wasn't being very convincing.

"I'd like to believe you could hold this job for the whole summer," she said. "Maybe if you did, I'd start to really feel like you're getting it together."

Emily had this dreamy look on her face like she was looking right through the eighty-pound bags of cow manure stacked against the wall of the shed. "I don't know where we go next," she said. "We need to get unstuck." She looked at me significantly.

Was she hinting at what I thought she was? If I shaped up and held on to this job would I get a few more stamps on my passport?

"Come over here," she said, smiling, before I could think of how to ask her what she meant.

I didn't have very far to go.

But when we kissed, something funny happened. Before,

35

it was like I'd get lost in it? Gone to the world? Now, all of a sudden, I found I was reading the fertilizer bags instead:

WARNING: NOT FOR HUMAN CONSUMPTION. DO NOT APPLY TO WATER OR WETLANDS (SWAMPS, BOGS, MARSHES OR POTHOLES).

I tried to concentrate; remember why I liked her. I thought of what Dad told me once, "If it wasn't for your mom, I'd be a bum. You need somebody who helps keep you on the straight and narrow."

AVOID CONTACT WITH SKIN, EYES, OR CLOTHING.

And Emily, after all, was trying to do just that. Sure I should be applying for college—business college even. Sure I should be doing all in my power to keep this job so I could prove myself and eventually fulfill my fate by getting married to her. What could I have been thinking of to not see this?

WASH HANDS AND EQUIPMENT THOROUGHLY AFTER USE.

If *anyone* knew how to get real; if I could trust *anyone* to stand through the mush of my dreams to the solid ground underneath and get me moving again, that person would be Emily Johnston. In fact, she was my last hope.

KEEP OUT OF REACH OF CHILDREN OR DOMESTIC ANIMALS.

36

So I certainly should take her advice. After a while they would treat me better at work.

Maybe they *were* just testing me after all.

BUYER ASSUMES ALL RESPONSIBILITY FOR SAFETY AND USE.

6

The next day, half the cardboard was dry, but the ground must've been wet in a few places and the rest was still damp. The sun was shining strong, though, and steam was actually coming off it, so I figured it would all be dry by afternoon, and I left it. Meantime, Lou said that Spiro had another "special" for me.

Down in the catacombs of the place was a stockroom where old plumbing supplies—pipes, couplings, elbows, and other old junk—were kept. Heaps of this rusty, dusty stuff were all over the place exactly like—You ever read the story where this old lady has been living for years in a house with a banquet room all set for her wedding, which never happened since the guy took off?—Imagine that, except she was a plumber instead.

Spiro wanted me to sort and inventory all this moldering

38

mudge. It looked like I'd have to list some pieces by their names on the periodic table of the elements since they'd crumbled back into their original molecules. Lou gave me a yellow pad and one of those stubby pencils you get at a miniature golf course and said to get to it.

Took me until the afternoon to make a dent in the stuff. As I poked through it, getting all dirty and bouncing my head off the bulb that hung by a wire from the ceiling, I felt my eyes begin to sting.

I was beginning to see the pattern. Testing me? Hell, I could see they were only *using* me like the way the weird cleanup guy, Barney, used the ratty mophead he pushed around. When I got all worn out and dirty, they'd throw me away for a fresh kid.

I wondered what they might do with me next: wrap me in rags and drag me through the smokestack to wipe it out? Have me suck all the old asbestos out of the walls with a garden hose? How about climb up the flagpole in a lightning storm to rip the flag off its rusty pulley? I began to see that in spite of what Vinnie had said, maybe I *hadn't* hit bottom yet.

It was late afternoon when I squinted my way back out into the daylight to see how my cardboard was doing. As I walked out on the loading dock, though, I didn't at first know what I was seeing. It looked like brown snow covered the spare lot and had drifted in globs onto the chain-link fence. Then it hit me it was the cardboard! Or what was left of it anyway. Someone must've driven a truck around on it,

39

mashing it all up and spraying the soggy wads all over the place.

Lou came up to me and, looking over his shoulder, said in a low voice, "Boy, you really bungled it this time, Buddy." (Why couldn't I get anyone to call me by my real name?) He handed me a broom and shovel. "Better go and get that crap out of there before Spiro sees it."

So while everybody else was cleaning up to go home for the day, I was out pulling bits of wet gunk out of the fence links. When it was nearly five, I dropped my broom and started to leave. But as I got to the top of the loading dock, there was Spiro standing in my way.

"Not so fast, Thackeray," he said, giving me a look like I was used dog food floating in his punchbowl, "I don't want you out of here until you're finished."

Before I could even begin to say anything, he turned and left.

As I worked I felt more and more angry and confused. It was long past five, the usual quitting time, and most everybody was gone by the time I was through scraping up all the stuff and dumping it in a barrel. When I finally pulled my time card, I saw there was a note stapled to it:

I hope you didn't expect to get paid overtime for cleaning up your own mess.
—Mr. Spiro

Then I looked at the last time punched on the card:

Five on the dot.

Spiro had actually punched me out! This was it! The final straw. That hot feeling shot up my spine again to where I wanted to tear into something.

Crumpling the card in my hand, I stomped through the warehouse to the front offices, hoping that Spiro was still there so I could tell him what to do with it. By now I didn't care if I got canned and had to start applying to business schools, or if Emily might cut me off if I didn't, or what Mom or Mr. Reynolds or whoever might say or think.

But the offices were quiet and empty.

I stopped at one of the desks, found a pad ("OK Construction—Make Plans Today—Then Call OK!") and used my little golf pencil.

"Dear Mr. Spiro," I wrote in big, block letters, hoping the polite opening would fake him into reading the rest. Then I heard a noise and quickly looked around.

I didn't see anyone.

"You may think that I'm just some slob in off the street who couldn't do any better than to work for this poor excuse . . ."

Again a noise.

Then I noticed Spiro's door was half open. Damn! Was he still here? Now I could tell him in person. I started to walk in, but before I could touch the doorknob I saw her: A girl—maybe a year or so older than me—sitting in there all alone at a keyboard, her back to the door. Her hair was straight and plain and brown and hung to her shoulders. My heart knocked in my chest like a bottle bouncing around the bed of a pickup truck.

It couldn't be.

She suddenly stood and walked to a file cabinet. I ducked behind the doorjamb, but not before I got a good look at her. It was like somebody squeezed down on my eyeballs. Like I couldn't believe what I was seeing.

It was her.

But it *couldn't* be.

But it *was.*

She was so lost in her work, I was sure she didn't see me. She looked much older than the last time, of course, but it *was definitely her.*

And then, I'm not one hundred percent sure why I did it—my life would have been completely different if I hadn't—I crumpled up the note and dropped it in the wastebasket, smoothed out my wrinkled time card, and put it back in the slot.

7

Seven

HERE IN THIS long shot you see me turn the corner of the (now clean) wall of the warehouse.

Next, in the same shot, all the guys hanging out in front, talking and smoking, see me coming and suddenly scramble inside like there was a fire in their shorts they forgot to put out.

Then in a medium two-shot inside the warehouse, you see me talking to Lou at the stock table: "What, have I got a disease or something?" I'm asking him.

In the final panel, in close-up, Lou looks at me and there's the beginnings of what actually looks like a smile. "When they see you coming," he says, "they know they've got exactly ten seconds to punch in."

"You're out of here" was the first thing Lou said next day when I stopped at the stock table, piled high with half-filled orders.

I got a stab of panic. Was this it? Would I have to hang up my bucket and kiss my scrub brush good-bye?

Then Lou helpfully jerked his thumb over his shoulder to where the construction crews stood, waiting for their orders and supplies for the day.

"You're with me," said a guy they called "Cooney," who had a bumpy red nose and wore his grease-stained OK cap jammed down on his head. He handed me a box of nails and some drill bits and next we were off in one of the beat OK vans.

We cut up and down side streets, Cooney checking his rearview mirror almost constantly like he was trying to shake someone tailing us, all the scrap in the back crashing around like a boxful of Christmas decorations dropped from a third-story window.

Cooney seemed all caught up in the fancy driving and didn't seem open to any questions about what was going on, though I really didn't care anyway. It was just great to be outside and free, speeding around through the sharp-edged morning shadows instead of being stuck back in the damp, peeling warehouse.

After a while, Cooney began to slow down and relax and soon we pulled onto the main street of a nearby small town.

There, lined up and down the street in front of a diner, were all the other OK vans. Inside the place—the Cup'n

Spoon it was called—all lined up and down the counter, were all the OK workmen, laughing, trading jokes, punching each other in the shoulder, and calling to the waitress.

"Does Spiro know about this?" I asked, nodding my head at everyone sitting here instead of out on a job.

Cooney studied me for a second. "Sure," he said.

"He doesn't mind?"

"Here's how it works," he said, as he swallowed up a stool in his wide backside and I slipped onto the one next to him. "He doesn't pay us too much and we don't work too hard."

Without asking, an old guy in a baseball cap with a gray ponytail sticking out the back made a cup of coffee appear on the wet counter in front of each of us and spun around to knife two pieces of toast from the four that right that second popped out of the toaster, buttering them with the same knife and dropping them on a plate next to a couple of eggs he'd just flipped muttering from the grill.

I looked at the cup of coffee and then looked up and started to ask for tea instead. This is usually what I had at home in the morning—a habit my mom got from *her* Irish mom—but the way this guy had it all choreographed, it would be like standing up in the middle of a ballet to ask for a polka—so I dumped a lot of sugar in it and made like everything was fine.

"Gimmie a setup like that, Jake," said Cooney, pointing to one of the plates the cook was putting together. "Tell him what you want," he said to me.

45

"Same," I said trying to be cool. "Except you got raisin bread?"

It was like when the bad guy comes through the swinging doors and the piano player stops and everyone looks up from their cards. The whole place got quiet.

The man turned and looked at us. Cooney gave him the shrug that meant: Hey, *I'm* not responsible for him.

"Whole wheat?" said the man, looking at me with narrowed eyes.

"Uh. OK," I said.

Then everybody started talking and the piano player playing and the dealers dealing again.

"Hey, Cooney," a guy yelled from down the counter. You could barely hear him over the other talking and the painful squawks of the counter stools. "You still on that job on Pelham?"

"What's her name, Cooney? You find out yet?" said another guy before Cooney could answer.

"Yeah," said Cooney, to the second guy, "it's Fatima. Same as your wife."

"That's a big job all right," said the first guy as the second guy scowled and the others laughed.

Sitting on the end as I was, the others pretty much ignored me and I spent the time watching the guy behind the counter in his little dance. He was a study in form and grace. Never a wasted action. Filling a coffee cup from an open tap while he dropped a couple more pieces of toast in the toaster, then grabbing the cup before it overflowed, delivering it to the counter, and replacing it with another while he dragged some of the mountain of orange-looking homefries onto the grill with some bacon and a couple of eggs that were just setting up. Scooping them on a spatula, slipping them on a plate next to the toast that popped up right then, whirling around—the now-full second cup in his hand—he slid the cup and plate down the counter where one of the plumbers fielded them and dug in without a blink.

Here was a guy who seemed to have no problems with his job. Someday I'd have to figure out how he did it.

I usually didn't have the stomach for much of anything when I first woke up, and I'd scarf down something at my locker between classes later on—maybe some cold pizza. But by now I'd been up an hour or so and was happy when I heard the clatter of a plate and looked down to see the food was in front of me and my coffee had been refilled.

"Get that boat yet?" said a dark, curly-haired man who Cooney had called Klots.

Cooney was sipping his coffee, his plate already looking like the cafeteria floor after a food fight. "You want that jelly?" he said.

"Go ahead," said Klots.

Cooney got deep into spooning jelly out of the tiny packet, which looked like a small boat itself, in the ocean of his big mitt. "If you mean, am I having the nightmare where I bought that old square bathtub of yours, forget about it."

"I'm not selling it, I told you," said Klots.

"And I'm not buying it," said Cooney.

"So what *are* you looking for?"

"I don't know." Cooney crammed a whole piece of toast into his mouth.

"Well, here," said Klots, reaching into his shirt pocket, "I went down and checked on one of these last weekend." He pushed Cooney's ruined plate out of the way and spread a wadded-up brochure out on the counter. "Sixteen feet," he said. "Double hull, fiberglass, sonar, the whole ally-katoosh."

"Beauty," said Cooney through his mouthful of toast. "These guys offering any decent loan money?" He poked the rubber-stamped name of the company with a jellied finger.

Klots, wetting a corner of his napkin in his water glass, wiped the jelly from the shiny paper. "Pretty good," he said, and told him the percent.

"Course you got to pay it back, Klots," said the guy who had started it all with Cooney earlier and who I'd heard them call Santana.

"Plan to," said Klots.

"You hit the numbers?" said Santana.

"Nope," said Klots, "But I figure there'll be some big overtime once we start on the WoodLand contract."

"Which?" said Santana.

"On the old Harding Estate," said Klots.

I'd been only half listening, gone to the world around me as usual, but now they had my full attention.

Santana laughed. " 'WoodLand.' Is that what they're calling it this time?" he said. "If you're waiting on that, you're gonna be fishing off a pier the rest of your life."

"They still talking about developing that place?" Jake whipped around, a full coffeepot suddenly in his hand, filling cups on down the counter in one, near-continuous pour. "I must've heard it a dozen times, these big plans—condos, golf course, swimming pool. She's crazy. The woman who owns it? She'll never sell."

Cooney suddenly drained his coffee, putting his hand over his cup when he set it down. "Got his, too," he said, nodding at me, tossing down a few bills and making for the door. I grabbed the last wedge of toast off my plate and ran out behind him.

"Thanks," I said when we were out in the street. The big man nodded, staring straight ahead.

We drove a couple of blocks and stopped at a red light. Cooney still looking ahead.

"That seem like a pretty sure thing?" I said, "With the Harding Estate?"

He studied me again. "How come *you're* so interested?" he said.

"I don't know," I said. "It's not too far from my house," I lied. I didn't want to get into how we used to live there in the caretaker's cottage and everything. "What do you think?"

"About as sure as the sun coming up blue one day. Could

happen." The light changed and Cooney fixed his eyes back on the road, closing the subject.

Cooney hustled when he worked and I did the running, getting tools off the truck, pulling lumber off a pile that had been dropped on the lawn of the house where we were on a job. We installed a counter in one place. It wasn't so bad being in somebody's kitchen with all its foody smells, feeling like you were doing somebody some good.

Of course I wasn't the best at it yet. A couple of times Cooney sent me for things like a "reciprocating saw" or a box of drywall nails, and I thought I could bluff it out like I did on Mr. Weatherwax's multiple-guess history tests.

I guess I thought that maybe if I looked hard enough at all the strange things in the truck, little labels with their names on them might pop up. So I'd keep searching until Cooney would come out, shoulder by me, and say "Looking for this?" grabbing some weird-looking tool that looked like something a cowboy doctor would use to take out a horse's appendix.

After the last job, Cooney bought us a couple of sodas and we leaned against the truck, spitting on the ground and wiping our mouths on our sleeves. On the whole I thought I did pretty good for the first day.

Which is why I nearly lost it the next morning when I went to go out with the construction crews and Lou called me over.

50

"You're with me today," he said.

"*Inside?*" I said, loud enough that a couple of the workmen glanced over.

"Why?"

"You screwed up, is all Spiro said," said Lou.

"How?" I said.

"I don't know," Lou shrugged. "That's all he said." I was beginning to learn the way shrugs talked around the place.

I guess I had forgotten and enjoyed myself too much and had to pay the price. Why was it so hard for me to learn that work wasn't supposed to be fun?

I also remembered something my dad had said—a piece of advice from his many work experiences: "You can never be too sure who likes you and who doesn't and how this moves you up or down."

I looked over at the guys, especially Cooney, for some sign that they had done me in, but they were all tied up in reading their orders for the day and ignored me.

Lou handed me a broom. "The roof," he said, pointing up in case I wasn't sure where it was. "Take that shovel and a trash can too."

The tarpaper wasteland on top of the warehouse was where all the old junk in the area went to die. It was studded with a dozen or so ripped-open brown paper bags with sandwiches gone totally blue from mold and tiny mummy apples in them. (School kids again.) Also a broken lawn chair, dirty oil filters and other old car parts, a couple of pairs of worn-out sneakers tied together by the laces, rotten sofa cushions, a dead bird, and some stony mounds of dog crap—probably one of the owners letting his dog loose up here.

It was already beginning to get hot as I started scraping up all this crud. I heard the workmen's vans roar to life out back and watched over the edge as they shot off in different directions like ants off a burning log.

8

EIGHT

MY DAD SCOOPS me up in his arms like I am made of straw.

"You smell like when you dig in the ground, Dad," I tell him.

He says nothing and in the next panel in close-up, I say:

"And anyway, I thought you were dead."

"What a strange thing to say, Neal-o," he says. "Sometimes you make no sense. Come on, let's go take a look at that trail I was telling you about."

Next, you see here, he sets me down and we're walking along a trail on the estate.

"Where does this go, Dad?" I say.

Here's a close-up of his face and you can see he's looking ahead and doesn't answer.

In this medium shot you see the two of us side by side, but in the next, he's suddenly pulling ahead, moving out of the frame.

Next you get a reaction shot of me fearful and wide-eyed, and then you see what *I'm* seeing. Maybe it's the low angle, but he seems to have these outrageously long legs.

Now he's getting way ahead of me with the long steps he takes with these stilt-like legs and I'm walking as fast as I can and then here I'm running, but I still can't catch up with him.

I shout for him to wait up, but it's like he doesn't hear me and he turns a bend in the trail and when I get there he's gone.

I walk and walk and walk, calling out to him, but I can't find him.

I started having a lot of trouble with my classes in school after my father died. It all seemed so . . . well like with algebra. You pretend numbers are letters and switch them around every which way, then change them back to numbers when you're done again. Or history—even Mrs. Parini my *history* teacher said it was tricks on dead people. Or geography—lines on paper. You couldn't draw a map before there was something on the news and it changed.

I couldn't get past the fact that everything was fake.

Since the whole funeral thing I was having serious problems with fake.

For instance, they try to make you believe it's not hap-

54

pening by putting flowers all around to hide the coffin and making it look like a bed with a satin sheet and pillow and playing this music that's like drinking pancake syrup from the bottle. But there he was in this *box,* with *makeup* on his face, and his hair combed weird. I kept talking with him, thinking that if I could only get him to open his eyes and get up and walk out of there with me we could forget about the whole thing.

And afterward, everybody comes back to the house and sits around eating sandwiches and drinking beer and they even forget and start laughing sometimes like it's a party or something.

But then they leave and the house gets all quiet. Mom, who is OK up to then, suddenly puts her hands over her face and starts crying. She's like "Oh, I guess everything will get back to normal now. You'll go back to school and I'll go back to work and as far as everybody else cares, it'll be like nothing happened."

From that time on she seemed to get quiet; to study everything. She got harder and harder to talk with like she was already listening to someone who you couldn't hear. Maybe she *did* blame herself for making us leave the estate where my father was finally happy, I don't know.

The Harding Estate itself was no fake. It wasn't like one of those Shady Acres Estates, or something where you drive in and it turns out it's a trailer park. It was—is—this huge chunk of property with a hulking, spooky-looking mansion dropped in the middle of it and stables and cottages and all sorts of trails and bridges and barns and sheds sprinkled all over from a hundred years or so of people living there.

My mom and dad and me lived in the old ivy-crusted caretaker's cottage. Having us live there was a way to pay my dad less, since the rent was subtracted from his pay. It was also a way for Evelyn Harding—the old woman who owned the place—to keep the cottage fixed up, since this was part of the deal, although, as it turned out, home maintenance was not one of my dad's strong points.

"Your dad wasn't a nine-to-five kind of person," my mom told me one time when I got her to talk a little. Like me, it was years before she could say anything about him without bawling, though there was something else beyond the sadness, something that made her all the more unwilling to talk about that whole time we spent there.

But last spring, we were putting in a garden at the new place and Mom said she wasn't very good at it since Dad had been the *real* gardener in the family, and I saw an opening.

"From working on the estate?" I said.

"Oh, he worked as a gardener for a couple of years before that," she said, "for different places. He didn't stay at any one job too long, though." She didn't say "Like you," but the way she glanced at me, she might as well have.

"Why not?" I asked.

We were planting flowers in the strip of dirt along the edge of the driveway. Except for the tiny lawn in front, this was about the only place you could plant anything, the backyard being a covered-over parking lot.

"Well after he worked in a place for a while he would come home one day saying the boss had it out for him, or the other guys were talking about him behind his back and then he'd either quit or stop showing up and get fired."

"So how did he get the job on the estate then?" I asked, popping one of the flowers—which Mom called "impatiens"—out of the ice-cube tray thing it came in.

"He was doing a job for one of the landscaping companies," Mom said, gently taking the plant from me and poking it in a hole she'd dug, "and Mrs. Harding liked the way he took extra time to fit the stones together in a garden wall she was having built, although his boss didn't—that's what Dad said anyway."

"So we moved there?" I said.

"She got his number and called us up and we moved the next week."

"I loved it there," I said.

"Your dad did, too," Mom said. "He was his own boss pretty much, but it was hard for me in that little cottage with you just born and only one tiny bedroom—space heaters, no air-conditioning, mold and mice and bugs—and a snake got in once. The hot water always got all used up in the middle of washing my hair. . . . I guess you were too young to remember all that. Give me some of those pink ones," she said.

Mom was right. I only remembered the *feeling* of the place for the most part. After all, what was I, ten, when we moved out of there? I *did* know that the estate, rundown as it had been, was Disneyland compared to the crummy two-family house we moved into with its toilet paper square of packed dirt yard.

I remembered that from when I was a little kid, Dad would take me out with him in the woods that covered pretty much of the estate, leaving me sitting up in a stroller with some mint leaves to chew on or a stick to whack the ground with. When I got older, I'd help him planting bulbs or shoveling a bag of peat into a hole to plant a bush.

Other memories sometimes float to the top of all this soup of stuff. Not that I could always trust them.

Like early one morning, Dad took me to see one of the projects he was working on. He led me through an arch in a high brick wall that was all around the Big House garden.

In the middle of it had been a statue, all covered in vines and half tipped over, surrounded by a circle of dirt and weeds and a low stone wall. When Dad cleaned out the weeds he saw it was the pool of a fountain, so he dug it all out, patched it, and filled it with water, then cleaned and straightened up the statue. I could see from the back that it was an angel with its wings folded in tight and could hear water splashing as we got close.

Before we could get to it, though, a woman about my mom's age who I hadn't seen before was suddenly standing there at the archway and calling my father's name. "I'll be right back," he said. "You go look."

As I got closer, I could see there was a stream of water coming out from in front of the angel statue. When I got around the other side I saw the small, stone figure of a naked boy—in by the angel's legs—taking a whiz into the fountain, the water pouring out of him as the angel looked on smiling.

My legs stopped moving and I gawked.

How could this be?

A naked kid, about my size, hanging out for all the world to see?

And where was all this water coming from?

I could hear my father and this woman—who was she anyway?—talking boring grown-up talk in the background as I was trying to figure this out. I guess even then I was lost to things around me because I suddenly heard someone say:

"He's got a pipe in him. It was broke, but we got it fixed. All boys got them. That's what Grams said."

I looked around and saw a girl about my age playing with her dolls on a patio at the top of some steps nearby. Her back was to the light and she was staring down at me.

I felt like I was caught doing something I shouldn't be and my face got all hot. I didn't know what to say, so I slunk away back to my father and the strange woman.

"You like our fountain?" said the lady, smiling at me. "You have a good eye for things, I bet, just like your dad." She was the most beautiful lady I'd ever seen—next to my mom, of course. "I know what else you'd like," she added. "Come with me."

I looked at my dad and he nodded, and so I followed her out of the garden and into the Big House, finding myself in a cave-like, dark kitchen with a black monster stove with shiny golden pots hanging over it.

The woman had me sit at a long wooden table and gave me some cookies with big chunks of chocolate in them.

"You know your dad got that fountain working again for us; he's a genius in the garden," she said.

I nodded and ate my cookies.

"You'd do well to grow up like him," she said, going to the refrigerator and getting a carton of milk.

On the table was a big pad of paper, lying open with a few pages folded underneath. On the top page was a drawing of the pans hanging over the stove. I was amazed. How could someone take those things over there with all their reflections and shadows and different sides of them and somehow get them down on paper here? I put my hand on the page to see if it was really flat.

"You like that?" she said, scaring me so I quick pulled my hand away. "It's OK," she said.

"How did you *do* it?" I asked.

"You start by looking. Very carefully. Then you get your hand to move to the lines of what you see."

"My dad always says it's a surprise how much you can see if you just look," I said.

She laughed although I didn't know what was so funny.

"What do you see in this?" she said, setting the glass of milk in front of me.

"Milk," I said.

"Look," she said. "*Really* look."

Although I didn't have the words for it then, I suddenly noticed how the top edge of the glass, as it curved toward me, cut into the circle made by the top surface of the milk. I saw how this circle of milk was actually like a shallow saucer since it climbed slightly up the sides of the glass all around. I saw three tiny bubbles on its edge that looked like two eyes with a big round nose in between.

While I was looking, the woman started tearing the drawing of the pots and pans off the pad. The pages underneath had other drawings on them too—one of the salt and pepper shakers, another of a couple of lemons on a cutting board, another of a man's face.

"Hey, that's my dad," I said, as she set them aside.

She didn't say anything, but pushed the blank pad over to me and set down a couple of pencils next to my plate.

"You try," she said, placing an apple in front of me.

I started looking at the apple, then trying to move my hand to follow its shapes like the lady said. After a few minutes, the screen door banged and the girl who had been in the garden came in, dragging one of her dolls by its leg.

"Hi, hon," said the woman who must be her mother. "Sit down and you can have some cookies with our guest."

"Neal, this is Claire," her mother said as the girl sat at the other end of the table. I shyly glanced at her, while I kept my eyes for the most part on the apple.

"Say hello," said her mother.

"Hi," said Claire.

"Hi," I said.

Claire's mother made her a place at the table and gave her a glass of milk.

"My mom's an artist," Claire said.

I didn't know what she meant.

"She's the best draw-er," she said. "These are hers." She pointed to the drawings on the table. "She draws lots of other things, too," she said and started describing some of them.

Before she got too far, however, the old woman—Mrs. Harding—suddenly appeared next to the table. I'd been concentrating so hard on what I was doing I didn't see her until she was right on top of us.

"Claire," she said, interrupting her. "Why don't you come with me?"

I looked up at the old woman. She was frowning. I wondered if maybe I smelled bad from working with Dad in the garden. I sniffed my shirt.

"Does Neal have a pipe, too?" Claire asked the old woman.

"Never mind," she said, "come with me."

Claire looked at first as if she was going to try to get out of it, but instead she sighed and grabbed another cookie.

" 'Bye, Neal," she said.

" 'Bye," I said.

"Don't mind Claire's grandmother," said the younger woman, when the older woman and Claire were gone. She was looking over my shoulder now. "Concentrate on what you're doing. That's the key. Don't forget the spots," she added.

I'd never noticed the tiny specks of white in the red before.

Now I can't look at an apple *without* seeing them.

9

IN THIS SHOT you see me coming out the door of the Big House and walking down a worn side trail. From my point of view you continue down the trail to a clearing.

(Inserts of a squirrel digging in the leaves, a chipmunk shooting across the trail, its tail stuck up, a patch of daffodils stirring in the breeze.)

Still from my point of view, the camera pans the clearing, passing over a giant flowering plant growing at the clearing's edge, then comes back to focus on it.

You see me walk into the frame and stand next to the plant, which is twice as tall as me. Next, the camera in a continuous close-up shot runs up along the length of this plant showing the wide, hairy leaves that alternate up its stalk and stops on its long, spiky top all covered with raspy yellow blossoms that looks like the bad end of some medieval torture tool. You can see by my reaction shot that I'm all caught up in looking at it.

So next here I am, sitting in front of it, drawing away, close-up shots of me cut in with inserts of the drawing taking shape on the page.

In voice-over, you hear pieces of advice the woman gave me back in the darkened kitchen:

"People don't really look at anything anymore unless they want to buy it," she's saying. "It's because of the shopping malls. They think that everything will be set out there like shoes in a store window. But it takes effort to really see things; you have to get out there and look. Hard."

So I'm looking hard, when, from off-camera, I hear the jingle of a horse's bridle, which makes me quickly jump to my feet.

The camera focuses from a long shot and you see through the surrounding underbrush someone on horseback. I walk towards the rider and soon you can make out from my point of view that it's the girl, Claire—older now, again catching me unaware.

In the following scene close-ups of me and her alternate.

"What are you doing here?" she says, as if I'm somewhere I shouldn't be.

"Drawing," I say, holding up the sketchbook.

"Let me see," she says, staying up on the horse.

I step out of the woods onto the trail.

Birds are chirping in the background. Her horse stamps its foot and does that horse thing where it sounds like it's clearing its throat. She pats it on the neck and leans down to take the notebook from me.

As she does, there's a close shot of her taken from the ground. You see how high she is in the saddle. Sunlight bursts like tiny, silent firecrackers from the thousands of tiny holes in the roof of leaves over her.

"A common mullein," she says.

"What?" I say.

"The plant you were looking at. That's the name of it. But you got the leaves wrong."

"I don't think so," I say.

She swings down from the horse in one easy swoop and ties it to a tree.

"Here. I'll show you."

You see both of us side by side as we go back into the clearing.

"See?" She says in this medium shot from behind us as we stare up at the giant tropical-looking plant. "The leaves don't have stems like you drew here. They flow right into the main stem. That's so they don't waste water. When it rains, every drop runs right down to the roots; that's why it does so well in ground like this." Insert of the scrubby dry ground around us. "They're survivors."

A lingering close-up as she speaks shows her long, chestnut

hair, which is pulled back into a ponytail held with a red rubber band like you find on a bunch of carrots. She is a little bigger than me, being a year older. As she puts her hands back over her head to adjust her ponytail, you can see the muscles on her arms defined, probably from all her horseback riding, and through the T-shirt she's wearing, her budding breasts. She's a woodland goddess.

"You do draw well, though," she says. Her smile is in the major megawatt range.

"I work out," I say.

Her smile dims to night-light wattage.

"I mean I'm working at it," I say.

"Oh," she says, the smile coming back. "You'll have to try over that rise," she says, pointing to a nearby wooded slope. "There's a standing dead oak down there all wrapped up in trumpet creeper. It's beautiful."

"So are you," you hear in voice-over, but all I really say is "I'll take a look. Thanks."

There's a shot of her from my point of view, walking away to get back to her horse. But in a close-up, she turns and looks back over her shoulder before stepping back out of the woods and disappearing. You can hear her mount up and see a shadow of her through the trees as she rides off.

Cut to the kitchen door of the Big House, my dad standing next to it, a hammer in his hand. I come into the frame.

"How did it go?" Close-up of my dad smiling.

"What?" I say.

"Your drawing," he says.

"OK," I say, remembering the pad in my hand.

"Where's the rest of your drawing stuff?" he says.

Close-up of me looking back over my shoulder to the woods.

"Oh," I say.

The next Monday after scraping off the roof, I'm back at work putting in my time, running cartons of nails out to a truck when Spiro sticks his head out of the office area, points at me, and jerks his thumb over his shoulder. I don't mistake this for the hand signs that mean "I love you."

As I go into his office, I sneak a look at the girl with the chestnut hair who keeps working away as if I'm not there. All the while I'm trying to think What have I done lately? I hoped he hadn't found the sink I'd dropped and knocked a chip out of its corner. I thought the white correction fluid I'd swiped from Lou's counter was a good way to cover it up, but then Spiro happened to grab and shake the little bottle, and the top flew off, giving him a white scar across the top of his bald dome. He probably wouldn't have even suspected me if I hadn't busted out laughing.

"Where's the hand truck?" said Spiro when he looked up from some papers he was standing over.

"You didn't tell me . . ." I said.

L9

"To what? Use your common sense? Go get it!" He stood glaring at me, his soda can in his fist slowly getting narrower around the middle.

In the minute I was gone, somebody had taken it—probably Vinnie trying to screw me up—and I had to hunt up another. When I got back, Spiro was standing where I left him, looking at his watch.

"Break time, already, Thackeray?" he said. "I need this done today."

He wanted me to move a couple of old file cabinets so he could bring in some new ones that he wanted closer to his desk. I thought of asking him why he didn't just switch the drawers since all the cabinets were the same, but thought better of it.

"I'll be right back," he said, planting his can of soda on the desk and heading out to the warehouse floor, a bunch of papers crumpled in his hand.

I started to tip the cabinet, to get the edge of the hand truck under it, but the thing wouldn't budge. I looked to see if it was screwed down somehow, but finally realized it was just the pure weight of the thing. I finally pushed it hard and tipped it, but too much, so it bumped into the cabinet next to it, knocking the little nuts-and-bolts people all over the place.

"Be careful!" the girl said between clenched teeth as I scooped them up and put them on Spiro's desk.

At least she noticed.

I smiled at her, but she turned back to her work.

I muscled the cabinet over to where Spiro said he wanted it and came back for the second, checking to make sure there was nothing on top.

I gave the third cabinet a huge shove, but it must not have been as full as the others since I nearly knocked it over, grabbing it just before it hit Spiro's desk, but not soon enough to keep one of the drawers from rocketing through the little people on the desktop like a runaway dump truck down the main street of Nutsville. A cup of pencils and Spiro's open soda also went airborne.

The girl leaped from her desk, grabbing a box of tissues on the way, and began blotting up the lake of brown soda on the floor.

"Damn," I said, rescuing the little figures and shaking soda off them. "I'm sorry."

"You'll be twice as sorry if Spiro sees this when he gets back." She held up a soaked piece of paper by its corner the way Mr. Reynolds held up the job offer back in his office at school.

"He's definitely gonna boot my butt out of here, is what he'll do," I said, looking toward the door. I'm sure I had that same look a dog gets when you catch him with his snout in a pie.

"Don't just stand there. Catch." She tossed me a wad of tissues and I began swiping at the top of the desk, which had gotten sprayed with soda before the can hit the floor.

"These are all ruined," I said, picking up a printout all covered with numbers where it wasn't soaked with soda.

"Here, you finish cleaning up," she said. She sat at her computer and clacked at the keys and pretty soon the printer started coughing up more printouts.

69

"Get this mess out of here," she said, giving me the plastic bag from the trash can by her desk. I crammed the wet, brown tissues and soggy paperwork in it.

She took a quick look out the door.

"Uh-oh, looks like he's headed this way." She grabbed the papers from the printer, wiped the remaining soda from the desktop with the cuff of her blouse, and spread the newly printed papers around so they looked pretty much like they had before the disaster.

She stashed the bag of soggy papers under her desk, and I was putting the nearly empty soda can and the cup of pencils on top of the new printouts when Spiro popped back in. I quickly made as if I was taking a pencil.

"Playing office, Thackeray?"

"No," I said. "Just needed a pencil for writing up orders."

He looked at me like I was trying to sell him fish eyes for jewelry.

"Sorry," I said, and hustled the last cabinet into place.

Spiro began looking through the papers on his desk. He picked up his soda can and tilted it to his lips, but then suddenly stopped in mid-swig.

"Hey!" he said.

The girl and I both froze.

"Who drank my soda?"

"You said you were going to get another one," said the girl.

He looked confused for a second, then shook it off.

"Oh yeah," he said. "Right," and as he sat down heavily in his chair, I slipped out the door.

NEW CONDOS POSSIBLE FOR HARDING ESTATE

Negotiations are under way to develop the 525-acre estate of the late Evelyn Harding off West Main Avenue into a community of more than 500 luxury condominiums.

A spokesman for OK Construction and Supply Co., one of the main bidders for development rights, revealed preliminary plans today. He would not disclose the amount offered. The owner, Alice Harding, could not be reached for comment.

The plans show homes with deep lots, a community pool, tennis courts, a riding stable, and wide bands of park space.

The company is one of at least four bidders for the property.

The plans add fuel to years of speculation as to what would happen to the well-located, decaying property that industrialist Thaddeus Harding first built on in the 1920s.

The scenic, heavily-wooded land on the western edge of Marshfield is crossed by the Ojibway River and several deep ravines.

12

There It Was.

Not rumor anymore, but neat black lines of type on the front page of the newspaper that Mom was holding up in front of her. Right next to it was a picture of the rundown guardhouse next to the main gates, a new No Trespassing sign nailed to its door.

Let me tell you a little about me and the newspaper. The last thing I read in it with any care was my dad's obituary. It was just too depressing to see the same old ordinary things—kids burning down houses with lighters, smash-ups on the highways, guys with big hair getting elected, artificial organs being stuck in someone's body, planets in other galaxies being found, and all the rest—all going on in exactly the same old ordinary way, even though Dad's (and my) life couldn't.

As far as the newspaper went, his death was much less of a pain than the two-inch snow storm that was all over the front page the day he died.

But Mom read every little thing in it so carefully. It was like she was trying to make sure she didn't *miss* something—some small particular piece of information that would *explain* it all to her or something. It was tough to get her to finish a part so *you* could read it. Like right now, for example, as she sat across from me at the breakfast table scouring the first section.

I kept reading as much of the piece about the estate as I could see, while Mom, on the other side of the paper, ground away at her geezer grub—some cereal that looked like little bales of straw, and bran muffins you could use to sand the rust off lawn furniture. Stay out of her way after she took her last gulp of tea.

The article went on about the history of the estate and other big projects OK Construction had done and how the city had grown up around it and that the electric wires and water lines and all were there and how easy it would be to get ready like it was meat loaf somebody left in the refrigerator that you just had to warm up in the oven.

I had to read it two or three *more* times before it finally sank in.

This was *the Harding Estate* they were talking about for picking off nits!

"Neal, look at this," my mom said. I thought for a second she was reading where the article went into the inside pages, but instead, she folded the paper over, putting the comics page in front of me, tapping one of the cartoons with a polished fingernail. "You tell me now . . ."

It showed two old women with scarves on their heads looking at a tombstone in a cemetery. One was saying:

"Such a good man. Worked hard every day of his life so his family could have food on the table and a roof over their heads."

In the next panel, the other turns to her and says: "So what's this, early retirement?"

"Mom . . ." I start to say. "All they're saying is you work all your life and what have you got?"

"That's supposed to be *funny*?" she said.

73

This is another problem with Mom since Dad died. She's lost her sense of humor. Nothing is funny to her, *especially* things that are supposed to be.

"Well, maybe not so funny," I said, "but true."

"True?" she said.

Suddenly she fixed me with the All-Knowing Mom Look.

"Neal," she said, "is everything going all right at work?"

"Yeah, no problem," I told her. (How does she do this?)

"Are you sure?"

"Mom!"

I don't tell her much. Otherwise she gets all caught up in it and—who knows?—maybe she'd call up Spiro and bawl him out.

"I just worry," she said. "You're so much like your father at times."

"How?" I said, seeing another opening and changing the subject all at once.

She put down the paper and breathed out in a deep sigh.

"He had all these strange ideas," she said, "like instead of fixing something, he sort of just tried to make it go away. Like the toilet in the cottage."

"What about it?"

"Don't you remember with the bucket?"

It suddenly came back to me that the whole time growing up, we kept a bucket of water next to the toilet and dumped it in when we were through.

"Yeah," I said. "I thought it was because we were in the country or something, I guess."

"It was embarrassing. The house was a wreck. That's why we never had anyone over." She took a sip of her tea and set the cup down on the picture of the guardhouse in the paper.

"He didn't like work?" I said.

"Oh, no, he loved the gardening part, but he always thought you should do what you liked best and ignore the other complications of life. It was part of a whole big thing with him: people's TVs and cars and houses owning them since they had to work to keep them all running, and if you don't fix something and can't use it, soon you see you don't need it. He had a saying about getting rid of things you don't need. 'Forgive and get,' or something."

" 'Give and forget,' " I said, surprising myself with what sometimes floated to the top of the waste lagoon of my brain.

"At least with this place"—she looked around the little apartment—"Well, you could call the landlord."

A caretaker who didn't care. I could see the genetic tie.

"But he liked it there," I said. "Did you see this?" I moved her teacup to one side and pointed to the article about the estate.

"Yes," she said, glancing at it.

"What do you think?" I said.

"What's done is done," she said. "I really don't want to talk about it anymore. It was a long time ago." She took the last fatal gulp of tea and bolted for the bathroom.

It *was* a long time—six years now—we'd lived in this crummy two-family house, some old guy renting next door, where we traded sunlight shining off the stream behind the

75

cottage for sunlight glaring off the cars that drove by on the street, where Dad died on the orange shag carpet next to the bed.

But the worst of it was that I was no longer in the place where I had so many memories of him. It was like—you know how it's hard to remember somebody's face when they're not in front of you? Even someone you know a long time? Well, it was so long since I was there, that I started to forget about the place—the paths, the pond, the willow trees, the log bridge that crossed Snake Creek behind the Big House; how my dad and I would get up in the frosty mornings so I could rake leaves with him for a little while before school, or fish with him in the pond on late summer nights. Worse than that, it soon might not *be* there anymore, even if I wanted to see it again.

Of course it would be good if Mom was more help. She always acted so strange when I tried to talk with her about that time—like today. She never had much good to say about it. I mean, was having to wait to rinse the soap out of your hair all so bad?

So remembering my dad was starting to get like this old puzzle where you tape up the box, but every time you take it out, there's more pieces missing. Maybe that's what was in the back of my mind when I signed up for Mr. Bhandaru's film class. No matter how many times you watch a movie, every single thing in it is exactly the same each time. If my memories were more like a film, I wouldn't have to worry about losing pieces of him.

. . . . . .

When Emily and I next got together, I told her what I'd heard in the diner and seen in the paper about the estate. I said how I couldn't imagine this place of my memory and dreams being bulldozed over for apartments.

"Condos," Emily said, with that dreamy look again, as if she was only half there. "For *condo*-miniums."

"I don't even know *what* a *condo*-minium is," I confessed.

"Well," she said, snapping out of it, "it's *like* an apartment except you buy it so you can save on taxes."

I tried moving my face in a way that I thought would show that I understood. I guess it didn't work.

"Look," she said. "I'll tell you what. We did a project in the club on tax write-offs last term. I'll give you a copy and maybe we can talk about it." More and more lately she was trying to draw me into this faraway world of hers beyond the shed where she saw high finance and commerce and industry and where all I could see were the rakes and shovels hanging on the wall.

"Does it have lots of pictures?" I said.

Em shook her head. A lost cause.

You see, Emily has been planning since the time she divided into two cells to be a major chip in the computer of Our Nation's Economy. "Invest in a Condominium" was probably one of the first routines in her operating system. She was a prebusiness major and president of the YACs—Young Accountants' Club.

(Me, imitating a bird: "Yac, yac, yac."

Emily: "Come on, Neal. I'm *serious.*")

In addition to explaining tax breaks for condo ownership, she could tell you anything you cared to know about stocks, bonds, mutual funds, or investments in general.

That's "you" I'm talking about. 'Cause right after where I pop the trick plug on my Henny Penny rubber chicken bank? That's where I redline on the money meter.

"Neal," Emily was saying, "some of these things are important to know." She patted the back of my hand, which happened to be on her knee. Then she got quiet again for a while. I knew what was coming next.

"Have you given any more thought to what we talked about the other day?" she asked.

"About getting 'unstuck'? Sure," I said. And it was true, I'd given it a *lot* of thought, but I'm sure not the kind she was thinking of.

"So?" she said.

"The job is going fine," I lied. "I just know I'm serious about it this time."

"And after?"

"You mean college and all?" I said.

"I hope you're keeping your mind open to possibilities." She meant *practical* possibilities of course.

"Sometimes I feel my mind is so open my brains have fallen out," I said.

She looked at me. Her eyes were squinched up like she might start to cry.

"Neal," she said, "I want this—us—to work."

78

I didn't want to go where she was going. I tried a dumb smile.

"If you would just try . . ." she said.

"I *did* like Bhandaru's class," I said, grabbing for a dandelion as I hung on the edge. "Sometimes I think—"

"Bhandaru's? You mean the film class?"

"Yeah," I said. "I mean there might be something there."

"That's the one you have the incomplete in."

"All I have to do is the film," I said.

Of course.

A film class in which all I had to do was the film.

My father's son.

"He said I had the whole summer," I said. "And I like it. Film. I think maybe I could be interested."

"I'll tell you what," she said. She sat closer and put her lips in range. "Get your assignment done, you're going to have enough to do next year and can't afford to be fooling around with incompletes, but I *need* to see something *more* from you than just schoolwork. You hold a job out there in the real world for the whole summer and I'll take it as *something.*"

We kissed.

"OK. Sure," I said as soon as I came up for air.

11
ELEVEN

A few days later I worked up the nerve and hung around hoping to catch up with the girl in the office and thank her for helping me. I knew she usually stayed late—probably getting in overtime to pay some bills.

But I didn't see her and finally, with my feet complaining they wanted to be attached to someone who was off them, and my stomach telling me it was taco time, I went to punch out.

There was her card, still in its slot a couple down from mine—ours the only two left. I looked through the shop floor windows into the office area. No one. Maybe she forgot to punch out? But then from the women's bathroom, across from the time clock, I heard what sounded like a choking sound.

Then it got quiet. I went over and put my ear to the door. Maybe I should bust in and do the Heimlich thing to her?

Suddenly the door fell away and I fell right into her—Spiro's secretary. "You again?" she said, pushing by me, her eyelids looking like they were turned inside out and back again. "You know that box of tissues was supposed to last me until payday?" she said, holding up the wad of brown paper towels she was using to blot her eyes. "This is like sandpaper." She brushed past me to the time clock.

"Are you all right?" I followed her.

She pulled her card out of the slot and started to put it in the clock.

"Wait!" I blurted, as if I couldn't say anything once she punched out.

"What do I have to do to get you to leave me alone?" she said. She swung her arm as if she was going to hit me and I started to duck, but she stopped a quarter inch from my nose so that the big brown soda stain on her sleeve was all I could see.

"Look at this blouse," she said. "Look at it. The stain won't come out. It's ruined."

She punched her card and slotted it, turning away from me.

"I'm sorry," I said to her back. "I can buy you more tissues and you can get a new blouse. You just pick it out and give me the bill."

She ignored me and shoved at the door next to the loading bay. They gave us no keys, so after hours you had to use this door, which locked when it closed behind you. It was hard to open, though, and she kicked it, but it still wouldn't budge.

"Here," I said, putting my shoulder to it and popping it open, but it swung out too far, bounced back, and banged into her arm.

"Just leave me alone," she said, rubbing her arm. She shoved the door open again, stomped out on the loading platform and down the stairs.

"Wait! Wait up!" I shouted after Claire as she galloped past. She slowed and trotted her horse back to where I'd been standing at the side of the trail.

There's some things you pick up even as a little kid, and after the time in the kitchen that day when her grandmother gave me the Eyeball of Doom, I never did go near the scary old Big House without my dad.

Instead, Claire or I would be out on the estate somewhere and we'd kind of just run into each other. One day I showed her a fort that I'd dug into a hillside and covered up with an old door and then she came back with a couple of dolls to play with. I didn't know if I liked this so much.

On another day on Strider Pond, we floated little sailboats that we'd made of pieces of wood. She was fun to be with.

"What," said Claire, as she wheeled her horse around and got close.

"I want to show you something," I said. She swung down and tied her horse.

I led her back into the woods where a huge oak near the top of a rise had snapped off halfway up during a storm the past week. The top part was still all full of green leaves that hadn't gotten the news yet. It was leaning on the ground, still attached by some splintery wood to its base, which must've been ten feet up.

"Come on," I said as I walked up the branches, which made kind of ramps that lead up to the trunk.

"Wow!" she said when she got up to the top, sitting on the broad trunk, which was way high up off the ground. "You can see far from up here."

"Yeah," I said, "But here's what I wanted to show you." I picked up my drawing pad, which I'd left lying on the trunk when I heard her horse.

I flipped the pages over to a drawing I'd done earlier that day. I'd sketched it from memory of an image that had stayed with me. It was of a girl with long chestnut-colored hair, up high on horseback lighted from behind by hundreds of specks of light flashing through a backdrop of leaves.

"This is me," she said.

"What do you think?" I said.

"It's good," she said seriously. "But still not as good as my mom."

"I like your mom," I said. "Where is your dad?" I added. "I never see him."

"Mom sends me to visit him sometimes. He's in the city. I don't go there much."

"Doesn't he come here?"

"Mom says she doesn't want him to. She says that's why we came here."

"Oh," I said, remembering how they appeared out of nowhere one day maybe three or four years back. A car drove up; they got out.

She looked so sad. I had an idea. I tore the drawing off the pad, rolled it up, and put a rubber band around it from inside my backpack. "Here," I said, holding it out to her.

"Are you sure?" she said. She didn't reach for it, and I shook it a little.

"Here," I said again. "Yes, I want you to have it."

She took it and smiled.

Later, back at the cottage, I was watching a show on our old TV. The picture was so bad, it looked like 3-D before you put on the glasses and I was squinting trying to make it out. There was a pounding on the door and when I answered it, there stood Claire's grandmother, her face looking sunburned, the rolled-up drawing in her hand.

"I need to talk with your mother," she said quietly.

My mom had come out of the bedroom when she heard all the noise.

"Your son gave this to my granddaughter," she said, as if I'd given her a rusty chain saw. She talked to my mom as if I wasn't there.

My mother unrolled it and looked at it. "It's a drawing," she said.

"Please tell your son to stay away from where he doesn't

belong," Claire's grandmother said and before my mom could say anything back, the old woman left.

"You haven't been playing by the Big House, have you?" my mom said.

I said I wasn't.

"Well be sure to keep away from it," she said.

I swore I would.

12

TWELVE

The next couple of weeks at work are weirder than usual. I'm into the job, what? Half the summer by now? We're busy and I'm pretty much picking all the major orders. Turns out that Lou relies on *me* because by the time light rays travel from the order slips through the thick lenses of his glasses, it's lunchtime. And yeah they grab Barney—the old guy from the supplies room—to help once in a while, but if the bottle of firewater he hid behind the fire extinguisher was an order, he'd be handling twice as many. Most of the time he has to ask me where everything is anyway.

They even get Vinnie to pull some orders, and you could always track him to his hideout by following the trail of cigarette butts.

But the downside is this: by working well, I'm helping all

the more to wipe clean whatever small traces of memory of my dad that may be left on the estate. Follow:

I show up on time and give an honest day's work.

This helps improve the fortunes of OK Construction.

OK Construction becomes a little bit better company.

This makes it all the more likely they'll actually get the contract to tear down and pave over the estate and, like I said, wipe away any leftover clues of my dad.

So in spite of how hard I try to keep things on hold, and stop from losing pieces of him, every little thing—even stuff *I* do—seems to cause changes that in the end will make everyone forget him. I might as well try to stand still on an escalator. I've got to do *something.*

But what are my plays here? Do I quit and show Mom once again that I can't hold a job long enough for paint to dry? Show Emily I'm about as useful as a mozzarella hockey stick? Start applying for business schools; or, if I don't, get cut off from the one person in this world who, so far, understands me the best? (Even if the "me" she does understand is a lumpy work-in-progress.)

And, by the way, after the deed is done and I no longer get a paycheck, do I wind up flat-gumwad-in-the-street broke again?

No, there was no way I could talk myself out of it. I *needed* to stay.

So I put my shoulder to the hand truck, my foot to the cement, and my heart in the scrap bin.

Me against the world.

87

In that way it didn't feel much different than everything else.

I did find that after a while, I got pretty good at it. My art training from Claire's mother and the habit of storyboarding I'd gotten from Bhandaru made me pretty good at remembering how things looked and where they were and how they connected together.

So when I went searching for something, I pictured what it was and where it was and then played back the frames until I got back to where I happened to be standing. It was like playing a movie backward in my head. Sometimes when Lou himself couldn't find something, he'd come to me, and even the salespeople, when they needed something in a hurry, would grab me. I felt kind of proud about this.

Since things were suddenly going pretty smooth, I wasn't completely surprised one day after I clocked out to find my car wouldn't start. Lou had me stay after hours, finishing off a big order, and when I went out and turned the ignition key to the Mighty Road Wiener, there was a click and then, nothing.

The lot was empty, most everybody having beat feet out of there, except for whoever belonged to the old pickup truck at the far end back by the trees. I guessed I'd have to invest a couple of days' pay in a tow.

I was starting to walk back to the warehouse, hoping there was someone who would open up for me, when the door next to the loading bay banged open and Claire came flying out shoulder first.

88

"Hold it!" I said, hoping to catch the door before it closed, but it was too late since it already whipped back and slam locked. Like I said, they didn't give us keys, so it looked like my luck was about as drained as my battery.

"What is it now?" said Claire, about the same time she saw my car sitting there with its hood up.

"Nothing," I said.

"Good," she said.

She stalked right in front of me, taller in her dressy shoes, as I stood there stuck to the pavement. My mouth opened and at first nothing came out, but I kept forcing it and finally I squeaked:

"Could you give me a lift?"

She stopped and turned, her face blank.

I was right away sorry I'd said it, thinking she was going to come back and tear me a few spare nostrils.

But instead she thought for a few seconds, looking at my car.

"I suppose," she said.

Turns out the old pickup was hers. Up close you could see it was *so* gone it looked like she'd been driving it underwater and forgot to close the windows.

I climbed up in the lumpy seat next to her.

"Where to?" she said.

I was taking her in. All good-looking and dressed up for work, the battered roof liner of the truck hanging around her in strands like a veil.

I guess I was a little too long in saying anything.

"Where to?" she repeated, turning the key, the truck starting and running smooth.

"Just to a phone," I said.

She started to put the truck in gear, but seemed to think for a second and with the clutch pedal still down, asked, "What's wrong with it?"

"The car?" I said. "Battery. It needs a new one. I was trying to stretch it until payday."

"I have cables in back," she said, letting out the clutch pedal and steering the truck over next to my car.

I found the pair of rusted jumper cables in a corner of the truck bed wrapped around a shiny dented wheel rim, hooked them up, got in the car, and turned the key. Nothing.

"Try again," said Claire, sitting up high in the cab of the junker pickup and racing its engine so I was afraid pieces were going to fly off.

I tried, but still nothing, so I got out and began to jiggle the cables where they connected to the battery. Suddenly there was a spark and a "bam" and I jerked my head away, banging it on the overhanging hood.

"Aaaa," I said, not too loud, rubbing my head, trying to not look like such a dummy.

But she must've heard all the noise. "What happened?" she said, cutting the truck's engine and quickly climbing down to stand next to me.

"Are you OK?" Her eyes narrowed as she looked me over.

"Yeah, yeah," I said. "Blew what was left of the battery is all." I pointed to the engine compartment where the battery's caps had been blown off and a sizzling liquid was eating through the hoses and my shirt where some of it had splashed.

"You got some on you," she said. "Wait, let me get a rag." And she pulled one out from under the front seat of the truck and started wiping at my shirt, which already had a spattering of tiny holes that looked like cigarette burns.

"Look, you need to get that stuff off you. Let me take you home."

But as I climbed back up in the front seat of the pickup, I thought of home, where I might run into my mom or have to answer a phone call from Emily, and I said, "I know somewhere."

The Cup'n Spoon in late afternoon was a different place. There was no line of workmen at the counter, no waitress, none of the rattle and crash and yapping that made it sound like a dog pound at feeding time.

Jake looked like all his air had leaked out. He was kind of yellowish under the lights, sitting at the end of the counter—I'd never seen him when he wasn't standing—reading a spread-out newspaper. Although he helloed us friendly enough, and jumped up and got a wet rag to get the rest of the battery acid off me, at this time of day he didn't have the same spark.

I asked Claire if she would stay until the tow truck came.

"I guess," she said, looking uncomfortable.

“So how are things?” I said to her, once we were sitting in a booth and had a couple of cups in front of us. Trying for the casual approach here.

She said nothing, only sat looking at me as if I was a hunk of baloney she found in the back of the refrigerator and was trying to decide was any good.

“OK,” she said warily. “It’s been a long time.”

“Six years,” I said, “since we left.”

“I heard about your dad,” she said. “I’m sorry.”

“Yeah, well . . .” I picked up my cup of tea and looked at the circle it had made on the paper napkin, then put it down again. It was too hot.

“Your grandmother, too, huh?” I said. Mom had seen the obituary.

“A couple of years ago,” said Claire. “I wouldn’t be here now otherwise. Could never work while she was alive. She wouldn’t let me. Thought it was below the Hardings to work for an hourly wage.”

“Your mom still OK?” I said.

“She’s good,” she said.

I thought she wasn’t going to say anything else, but then she added, “I’m surprised to be talking with you like this.”

“I guess I am, too,” I said, “You were pretty upset the other day.”

“I was having a bad day already, and you weren’t helping,” she said.

“I really will pay for a new blouse,” I said. “You just tell me—”

"It was just a bad day," she interrupted. "We had a tree branch wreck the porch roof and the insurance that Grams had didn't cover it and . . ." She let it trail off. "I guess I shouldn't have snapped at you."

Neither of us said anything for what seemed like a long time. "How is the place?" I finally said. "Except for where trees have fallen on it?" Fishing for a laugh. She wasn't biting.

"You wouldn't recognize it. Everything is all overgrown. You know like those Aztec ruins they find in the jungle?" she said. "After you guys left, my mom and Grams tried to do it all on their own, and now with Grams gone . . ."

"And your horses?" I said, not thinking how this would be a touchy topic.

Again she gave me a wary look.

"I've been able to keep one," she said. "Takes a good part of my pay for a week to keep her fed and get all her shots and everything, but it's worth it."

"You still like riding?" I said and before I could stop myself I blurted out: "I'm sorry for what happened, you know. I never had a chance to tell you."

"It was a long time ago," she said.

"I didn't know how to talk to you afterward. I was still a little kid, and then we moved nearly right away and my father died and all. . . ."

"Let's not talk about it," she said. I would have liked it better if she said, Let's forget about it.

"OK," I said.

I tested my tea with a small sip. It was cool enough so I

93

drank more, trying to cover up the silence. Finally something hit me. "Oh yeah," I said, "I saw in the paper about the plans—for the condos and everything? What's that all about?"

"Well, when I started working here and they found out where I lived, they wanted to talk with my mom. I guess they made her a good offer."

"So she's going to sell?"

"Well, don't believe the newspaper; there's a couple of other places interested and she still isn't sure. I don't think she really wants to; I really hope she doesn't. I don't know where I'd ride, or keep my horse, but the place is too expensive to keep. Mom's been showing me the taxes."

"There's so much of it," I said, "Couldn't she sell off *part*?"

"I don't think so," she said, "something about the trust money that my grandfather left to keep it up—that we can't sell off pieces or something. She's talking to a lawyer. I'm sure he never imagined the money wouldn't be enough."

The light from the late afternoon sun was climbing up the wall behind her. "Look," she said, antsy all of a sudden, "I've got to go. Maybe you better check the tow truck?"

"Oh, yeah," I said. I'd forgotten all about it.

As I stood, I grabbed at a napkin from the holder on the table and knocked the salt and pepper and sugar holder flying. The shakers clattered on the table and the little packets of sugar spun everywhere and she jumped.

"Sorry," I said.

"That's OK," she said, fumbling for her keys, not looking at me. "I really have to leave."

"Go ahead," I said. "I'll get a ride."

She dropped some money on the table and walked out, disappearing into the low sun coming in through the front door.

In the last years that we lived on the estate, I was old enough to go anywhere on the property my imagination led me (except near the Big House, of course) and do about whatever it suggested. Usually it suggested things like trying to make a bow and arrow out of a bent tree branch, hunting up new things to draw, tracking a raccoon, trying to train a squirrel to come get a peanut—something lame and tame. But one day it led me to copy something on TV.

In the show I'd seen, some villagers who lived on the edge of a jungle in India were being picked off one by one by a tiger. He would sneak down from the nearby mountains at night and claw through the straw roofs of one of their huts. The next morning when nobody came out, someone would get up the nerve to peek in and all they'd find is table scraps.

So to catch the tiger—they showed exactly how they did it in the film—they dug a pit and covered it up with brush and leaves and dirt. Then they hid in some trees nearby, and when the tiger fell in they leaped down and swarmed around the pit and killed it with spears and rocks and whatever else they could get their hands on.

95

Well, one day not long after I saw this, I walked off into the woods with one of my father's shovels over my shoulder. It wasn't so long before we left the estate, so I must've been about nine years old. I had already burrowed out an underground fort, like I said before, so my father didn't think anything of it.

I dug out a pretty good-sized hole that day right in the middle of one of the trails that nobody ever used much. It took me until it was nearly dark to finish and it was so deep that from down in it, I could barely see over its edge. I covered it all over in brush and leaves and dirt like on TV and then went back to the cottage to bed.

Don't ask me what I was thinking. The closest tiger was in a zoo a hundred miles away and if it escaped and fell in my trap, I wouldn't have known what to do with it. I think I just liked the idea of having a reason to sit up in a tree and look around, and an excuse to do nothing in the meantime. The next morning, I even brought my sketchpad up the tree in a backpack and did some drawings of what things might look like to a squirrel.

About halfway through that morning I started getting tired of having to balance myself in the tree to pee. I thought I'd climb down and go see what my father was doing and maybe get something to eat.

I was starting down the tree, concentrating on my handholds and where I put my feet, branch by branch, when I noticed . . . you know the way you all of a sudden hear a faraway train on a quiet night?—I heard the familiar sound

96

of a horse's hooves galloping along the trail. I started thinking how it always sounds like they have three legs instead of four if you listen close? (Tap your fingers and see for yourself.)

Then I thought: It must be the girl, Claire, out riding. Great! Maybe I could get to talk with her away from the grandmother, and next—as if my wish somehow caused it—I see she's coming right *toward* me, and I'm thinking I only have a few more branches and I'll be down, and next I'm thinking:

THE HOLE!

Damn it!

I'd better warn her not to . . . and as I come to the next-to-last branch I hear she's getting way close and I shout out, but I'm still all caught up in the tree so it must've come out like I was rolled up in a mattress or she probably didn't hear anything over the horse's snorting and hoofs, so I skip the last branch, take a major leap to the ground, and fall with the wind half knocked out of me, running out to stop her, but she's moving fast and all I do is scare the horse, who jerks his head to one side to see me with his one big, milky eye, and the girl way up there on his back looks down at me scared, too, and next—galloping by me—she *still* might have seen it if I hadn't been there yelling like an idiot—the horse steps into the pit I've dug and goes down and—I get to see all this up close—she goes airborne over the horse's head and lands Cluuump! on her shoulder and neck and lays there.

I run to her past the squirming horse, who didn't fall in the hole all the way—only one of his legs. He's snorting heavier than ever and trying to get up, but kind of going in a circle the way Curly in the Three Stooges does, laying with his ear to the ground and trying to run. When I get to the girl, she's moaning and only half there and I say "Wait, I'll get someone," as if she's going somewhere. And she looks so *small* on the ground there.

"You," she says, looking up at me.

After that it's all blur time. Crying. Running to get my father. Trying to tell him what happened. Running to the house and telling her grandmother—all huffy to see me there at first—to call an ambulance. Going back out there with my dad, trying to keep the girl quiet when all she wanted to know about was her horse.

"Scotty. Scotty," she kept calling, although not too loud—her couple of broken ribs kept her from shouting much.

The ribs and her arm and her collarbone—that was the major hurt she had, and they had to carry her out of there, around the still-floundering horse, on a stretcher.

The horse—her favorite, I later found out—they had to put down.

They used a needle as big as a bicycle pump and injected something into him and he got quiet fast.

This is what I remember next, and is my strongest picture of all the things that happened that day, although the whole thing was too awful for me to even think about storyboarding: the horse's long, beautiful head hanging off the tailgate of the pickup truck—its bed not big enough, but the only thing they could fit down the narrow trail, and that with backing it a quarter mile—as they hauled him away.

After that, the girl didn't need her grandmother getting in the way. She made it her own personal rule never to speak to me again.

13

THIRTEEN

"IN THE FIRST panel you get this head-on view of some big snot-blowing bull chewing up the turf as he charges the camera.

"Next here's me looking way surprised and leaping to my feet and running. As I glance back, you see in this series of shots from my point of view that the bull covers an incredible amount of ground in an incredibly short time. Here's my reflection in his eyes in this extreme close-up."

If you could get close enough to Emily, you could see my reflection in *her* eyes as I show her this latest of my movie storyboards, this one of a dream I'd had. If only I could convince her how doing this is important to me . . . get her to understand.

"THEN HERE'S A wide-angle view, shot from the side, showing me running from the bull, his horns lowered like he's going to dig into my butt.

"But since this is a dream, next time I glance back, instead of the bull's horns, you see the grill on the front of an old pickup truck and then, in another flash, it's a horse—someone's on a horse galloping right up on my tailbone, trying to ride me down.

"But next my feet bog down in that old slo-mo dream swamp, which probably even ancient Egyptian mummies dream they're slogging through—a quick cut to me getting nowhere—flat-looking like one of those pyramid drawings, a flat Egyptian bull behind me.

"Then cut to my view straight ahead—now you can see my father's head and shoulders up there up above the tree line. I know he can save me and I run and run, getting closer and closer to him.

"Next I break from the trees, expecting to see him in front of me, but he's somehow blended into the garden wall. He's made of—or part of—the brick, his legs spread out over the arched doorway to the garden, his head stony with a wreath of leaves on it ('Don't ask,' I tell Emily. 'I didn't make this up; it's a dream.') but I know that however he's changed, once I get through the door he's guarding, I'll be safe.

"I rush in and slam it behind me and next there's a close shot of the door and you hear a huge thud and you see it bulge and go back again, the dust falling out of its cracks. But it holds.

101

"Then cut to me in a bed in the garden sitting bolt upright like I was sleeping and the blast from the bull woke me up. It's morning and I open the garden door and go out, expecting to see my dad up there keeping watch, but instead you see that it's only the ordinary wall again.

"I search around in the woods for him, then you see in a close-up, how I'm kind of creeped out looking over my shoulder like there's still something lurking to get me, so I start to go back in the garden where it's safe, but when I get there you see that there isn't even a door anymore.

"I feel along the wall hoping to find it, but now it's all just a smooth brick skin. There's no way in. In this final close-up here, I put my cheek up against the cool brick and close my eyes as the scene fades out."

"Interesting," says Emily, giving it the Kiss of Apathy.

She pauses and adds: "But I thought you told me your movie was going to be about your *memories*."

"I know, I know," I say, "but this was so *strong*, and I *knew* it, like I had the same dream before, and dreams are a kind of memory, too, so I'm thinking about adding it in."

"Oh," she says. "I guess I don't really understand this whole film thing."

It was dusk and we were walking around the streets near her house. She said that the shed was off-limits since her dad was in and out of there a lot hauling out blowers and rakes and other weapons in the Fatherly War on Grass, and Emily had made it clear she would never set foot in my junker car.

"I don't know if *I* understand it all yet," I say. "Bhandaru told me once to not think about it and go with my feelings, and I've been playing around with that."

"Your feelings?" she says.

"Bhandaru says that's the best way to *start,* anyway."

In front of the mirror at home, I'm always very brave when I practice breaking the news to Emily that I'm changing—getting farther and farther away from her idea of Who I Am. But when I'm standing right in front of her? I always backpedal.

"It's not only film," I say, blundering on, "I've been kicking around some other ideas, too."

"Ideas?" she says. "Like what?"

"Ideas like art," I say.

Where did I get *this* from? Oh, I know, I'm trying to dig myself an even *deeper* hole by coming up with yet something else that Emily will think is even *more* impractical.

More no response.

"Remember how I told you how I had a sketchbook when I was a kid, and how I won stuff in school?" I said.

"You were great," she said. "I remember Miss Carnet had you show the class up on the board once how you did trees."

"Yeah," I said, "Draw along with Neal. Just follow the bouncing chalk."

"You were good."

103

"I liked it, too. So that's what I mean. If I could . . ."

"I don't know, Neal," Emily said. "I think you need to come from a family that has money if you want to do something like that. I saw on TV that van Gogh sold only one painting in his whole life."

"So he should have been a dentist?"

She punched me in the arm.

"No, I mean you've got to think down the line to things like supporting yourself and . . . others, maybe. It's not like food grows on trees."

"Some of it does," I said.

"You know what I mean," she said.

We walked silently past a few houses. It was getting dark and you could see people walking around inside the lit rooms. I found myself looking in at them, wondering how *they* had managed to get through all this and somehow find what they wanted to do with their lives. I wasn't looking where I was going, though, and stepped off the curb, nearly losing my balance.

Emily grabbed my arm and pulled me back up on the sidewalk closer to her. "You're such a dreamer," she said, putting her head on my shoulder.

"That's what my mom says, too," I said. "That I'm a dreamer just like my dad. Except she always shakes her head when she says it."

"It's nice to dream," says Emily. "It's fun, but you know what *my* dad told me once? 'There's no such thing as good dreams; there's only good deeds.' "

And a stitch in time keeps the breeze off your butt, I thought. But I didn't say anything.

"You know," Emily said, after we walked for a while, "you don't even have to really know *what* you want to do if you start out in a business program. People will see it on your résumé and that's all they need. Even if you decide to go into something else."

I hoped she couldn't see the face I was making in the dark.

Why did it have to be so hard, lately—talking with Emily? The way I had to be constantly on guard about what I was saying and forever thinking ahead to my next move? It was starting to seem like playing poker with both my hands stuck in bowling balls.

Part of the problem was that she knew all about me, of course, from being together so many years. I couldn't put anything over on her.

Part of it was Emily, herself. Even when we were kids and our parents used to visit, she had all these rules about how you actually played with things and how you had to put everything back in its box when you were through—she made her mother save the boxes things came in.

But there was another piece of it that made it especially hard, especially lately.

I felt I was starting to change—don't ask me exactly *how*. That's part of changing—you *don't* know. And it's hard to change when you're with someone who knows you so well. Everything you say, every little action, keeps you the same kind of person you *were* instead of that new person you want

105

to be. It's impossible to break away and be yourself—your new self—whatever that self might turn out to be.

One thing that talking with Emily was still good for, was that it made talking with Claire seem so easy.

First of all, I should say we *had* been talking more—Claire and me.

You see, I stayed late waiting for her the next day after my car died. I stood there in the parking lot with the hood of my car wide open—should I mention this was *after* I had it fixed?—where I knew she had to pass by. And, sure enough, after I was standing there only a few minutes, she came out.

I quickly ducked under the hood and started jiggling the tangle of wires and hoses as if I really knew what I was doing besides getting grease on my hands.

"Again?" she said, when she got close.

"Oh, hi," I said, all innocent like. "No, it's working fine—only a new battery like I thought. I was only checking it out."

"Good." She hesitated a second before moving on and I saw an opening.

"Claire," I said.

She stood there, the sun getting down behind the trees at the edge of the lot, backlighting her like that time I saw her in the woods on horseback. It took me a moment to find my voice again.

"Yes?" she said.

"How's that truck of yours working?"

(I know, pitiful flopping around like a bug-eyed fish.

But here, *you* come up with something quick: “____________________”)

“OK,” she said, barely moving her lips.

She started to turn but stopped. “But I am a little worried,” she said.

“Why?” I said.

“Well, I’m supposed to haul in some hay over the weekend, and I don’t know if it’s up to it.”

“Maybe I could help,” I said. “I could follow. I mean in case you broke down or something. Think of it as a payback.”

She considered.

“Yeah, I guess it would be good,” she said. “I probably need some help getting it in, too. I was worried that my mom might try to help and her back isn’t good.”

“So when?” I said.

“Saturday, I guess.” She gave me directions to a place out in the country where she would pick up the hay.

“Is nine OK?”

“I’ll see you then,” I said.

“Good,” she said.

It may have been the shadow of a tree branch she walked under, but I thought I saw the slightest of smiles cross her face.

14

FOURTEEN

Next Saturday found me following Claire's rust-munched pickup, its bed piled high with hay bales, the staggering load causing bigger-than-usual clouds of blue smoke to billow from under it so that driving behind it was like driving in fog.

Now that it was really happening, now that I was really going back on the estate to see the places where I roamed as a kid with my dad, I felt kind of scared. Mostly I was afraid my screwy moviedreams would bust a reel and get all snarled up in the face of what I really *would* see: Maybe the Chasm would be just a ditch, the garden only a cement bench in the middle of a bunch of dead weeds, the Big House some old dump.

Maybe, instead of some powerful figure with long legs or golden wings, I'd find my dad was just another old fart you would pass in the street and not think of anything except Where do they get those old-fart clothes? You know, plaid Bermuda shorts hiked up to the armpits, sandals with black socks, golf shirts with pictures of little squirrels on them?

Then there was Claire's grandmother—gone now, but probably haunting the place. I *still* had pictures of her in my head like when you see something in a cracked mirror: standing with her arms folded, frowning, as my father and I leave Claire's mother's studio. Red-faced as she hands my rolled-up drawing to my mom. And another, even stranger, of her storming in the cottage door, shouting, the day before all of us left the estate for good.

This last scene really weirded me out. Afterward, when I asked Mom about it, she brushed it off, and then we moved and Dad died and it seemed connected to that, too, somehow and became something I wasn't even going to ask her about anymore. Even now, when I tried to tell her where I was going, and who I was planning to meet, she looked kind of startled at first, then didn't want to hear anything about it. You would think . . .

So what *was* I doing here now? Maybe I should be happy with just remembering the estate and my father the way they safely *were.* Maybe I should be concentrating more on the present where it was plain to see that I needed a lot more work.

Here, for instance, driving right in front of me, was the very-much-in-the-present-not-a-ghost Claire. I wouldn't mind figuring out how to spend more time with her, although I had the slightest spasms of guilt when I thought about Emily and our unspoken promises.

But, get a grip. I'm only helping Claire out; paying her back. Really! There isn't anything more to it. Right? (Blink if you can hear me.)

I followed Claire in through a side gate and down a road where I had to dodge both the potholes and the chunks of her truck that were flying off.

Medium, moving shot: Through the yellow rental van's windshield you can see the three of us—my father driving, my mother with her arm around me. You see us bouncing up and down as we hit the potholes and hear our stuff rattling around in back.

Close-up on me and my mom:

"Why are we leaving, Mom? Where are we going?" I say.

"Your dad's got a new job," says my mom.

"What is it, Dad?" I say.

Close-up on Dad in profile: he has black circles under his eyes, his hair is messed up, he hasn't shaved.

"We'll see," he says. "We'll see." He keeps his eyes locked ahead.

Already I'm having problems making what I'm seeing fit with my memories of the place. The fact that everything looked very different from behind a windshield didn't help. When you walked through somewhere, everything was one-of-a-kind, *this* tree, *that* flower—*this* clump of bushes, *that* rock. But now it was more like scenery—like maybe what they show at the beginning of a movie? Things just slid over the windshield.

In a few short minutes we were in front of the Big House. Everything was smaller and closer together than I remembered.

I got out of my car and, leaning on the open door, looked up at the house. I saw right away that a *lot* of things had changed. It looked all fuzzy as if my eyes were watery. The paint peeled like a bad case of sunburn, leaving big splotches of naked wood, except for one side, which was a different color and badly faded. Shutters hung by their corners where they hadn't fallen off. One of the gutters hung crossways like the red "no" line in a No Parking sign. A chimney had fallen over, drooling a line of bricks down the roof. Part of the porch roof was collapsed and a tree limb leaned on it.

It was like one of those "Find-twenty-things-wrong-with-this-picture" games in a kid's book.

Claire was checking a rear tire on the truck when she saw me frowning.

"I don't know what happened," she said. "Your dad painted the house last thing before you guys went away, but the paint all started peeling off in a year—except for there, of course," she said, pointing to the faded side. "He never did get to it."

I started to have second thoughts about this whole thing and was on the edge of getting in the car and leaving, but by then, Claire, satisfied that the tire was OK, ran up the front steps. She pushed through the front door and I followed.

Even though it was midmorning, the downstairs of the Big House was gloom dark. We passed through room after dark, empty room. As we started to walk down one long hall, though, you could finally see light. It was streaming through the thin curtains that covered a couple of glass-pane doors at the far end.

Claire went up to the doors and knocked.

"Mom?"

I felt my guts tighten.

You could hear a chair scrape inside and footsteps. A woman came to the door, pushed the curtains aside, and peeked out, then opened one of the doors. It had been years since I'd seen her—Claire's mom—and last time I was a kid.

Her face was something like Claire's but longer and her hair graying. She had Claire's liquid brown eyes, and the same drop-your-doughnuts beauty she'd always had and which Claire inherited. There was something about the way her nose and mouth and eyes and hair were all put together that made you keep looking.

I couldn't figure what it was when I was a kid, but I think I've finally worked it out:

With most people you find something wrong—their nose is a honker, or they have a hairy wart on their chin—and you're kind of—what can I call it?—relieved: "Hey, here's somebody who's a regular person [funny-looking] just like me."

But with Claire's mother, there *wasn't* anything—she was perfect, and you just kept looking and looking, like one of those spinning spirals that sucks you in farther and farther. She must've been used to people staring at her.

"Claire," she said, "you didn't tell me you were bringing someone."

"It's just for a while, Mom, I needed some help."

I smiled and waved.

"Why, it's little Neal," she said, opening the door wider and unloosing a smile that was clearly the mother of Claire's.

I usually don't take well to being called "little" *anyone,* but this lady could call me Little Bo Peep if she wanted.

Through the open door, I could see a big, cluttered room, which—I had a murky memory—was her studio, with windows all along one side like it used to be a porch. A couple of big tables and a dozen or more easels—each with a square of canvas on it—filled the place.

"Yeah, hi," I said, not saying anything else so I wouldn't say anything stupid.

"How is everything?" she said.

"Good," I said, hoping she liked a man of a few words—a very few.

"You've settled in where you are?"

"Oh, yeah," I said. "We've been there a long time now."

"Six years," she said.

"Yes," I said, "six years."

"Well, it's good to see you, but we'll have to talk some other time. I'm working now, dear." Her mom said this more to Claire than me. "Why don't you and Neal get yourselves something to eat. Make him feel at home."

"And that's Mom," Claire said a few minutes later, as she busied herself in the house's wide, dark kitchen. "I don't know how much you remember her."

Remember her? Claire's mom was my first Fantasy Babe.

"Pretty well," I said.

"Kind of hot weather for soup," Claire said as she put a Flintstone-sized bowl in front of me. We were sitting at the big table in the kitchen where we first sat when we were kids and Claire's mother introduced us. "But the kitchen garden is in," Claire went on, "and so much is ripe; it's such a great way to use all the stuff."

The bowl had a load of vegetables treading in the broth: carrots, potatoes, string beans, peas, and some that I'd never heard of that Claire named for me—cilantro, kohlrabi, rutabaga.

Most of the vegetables we ate at home these days came from the supermarket where they had both types: lettuce *and* tomatoes.

"What kind of soup *is* this?" I said.

"We call it 'stone,' you know, like from the kids' book?"

I must've given her one of my award-winning blank looks.

"People in a town can't stand to see someone cooking soup with just stones in it," she explained, "so they wind up giving what they have—celery, carrots—whatever. That's what Mom calls it anyway—she just throws in stuff."

"This is good," I said.

After we lugged the hay up into the stable loft and she introduced me to her horse ("Howdy, Hester! Nice nostrils."), Claire and I walked one of the trails.

"Don't take my mom wrong, by the way, she's like that to everybody. Nothing gets in the way of her work."

"No, that's fine," I said.

"Well, what do you think about the place?" she said, "Does it look much different to you?"

"For starters," I said, "It looks like you shrunk everything by a third."

She laughed. "And it's all pretty rundown, right?" I was glad *she* said this.

"I guess," I said.

"Ever since you guys left, like I told you, we tried on our own, but it got too much, especially after Grams died. My mom got pretty good with things—you know, fixing sinks and stuff—after a while, but she finally decided it was taking too much time away from her art."

"What about the garden?" I said, remembering my dream garden whose wall I'd seen on the way into the Big House.

"I'll have to show you that, too," said Claire. "Grams

always kept it locked up before she died, though—to keep out the deer and rabbits, she said—and she put the key away somewhere. I haven't even thought of it lately. I'll look for it."

She walked me around showing me all the sites—Strider Pond, Snake Creek, even the Chasm, which hadn't shrunk by nearly as much, I was happy to see.

We soon found ourselves in one of the bigger clearings. I recognized it as the one Dad used to call the Sea of Tranquillity—like that huge, flat, open crater on the moon?

"This is one of my favorite spots," said Claire.

An old wagon with flat rubber tires sat in a pair of ruts in the middle of the clearing. Claire climbed up in the seat and I got up beside her.

It had started to get summer dark—so late it should be night, but the sky stays day anyway? This sky was all different ways—sunny but hung with clouds like one of those textbook pictures with all the kinds in it, like it didn't know which way to go.

We sat looking ahead at the ruts that faded to the edge of the clearing.

"Can you imagine tearing all this up for houses?" I said.

"No," said Claire. "This is the only place I remember living." She looked behind us and then ahead. "The main road would go through here."

"Right through the Big House," I said. It was directly beyond the trees.

"Is that what you called it? 'The Big House,' " she said.

"Yeah, my dad had names for everything."

"Everything?" she said with a slight smile. "What did he call me?"

"Norma Jean," I admitted, leaving out "The Wild Wood Queen" part.

She laughed and seemed to loosen a little. "From what I remember, he was a nice man," she said.

"What *do* you remember?" I said.

She told me how he nursed plants that they'd given up on—poinsettias from Christmas, hyacinths from Easter—back to health in a "plant hospital" he'd set up in one corner of the greenhouse and how he'd replant them in big, shallow pots, which he'd give her mother on the holidays—"for the house." How Claire brought him a cardinal one day that had smashed itself into a window, and how he found a box for it and fed it until it was strong enough to fly again. How he was always so generous.

"I remembered he always used to tell me to share stuff," I said. " 'Give and forget,' is how he put it. I was just telling my mom this a week or two ago."

"I guess I even played like he was *my* father sometimes," said Claire.

"What happened to him?" I said. "Your father."

"He's living somewhere with his new wife," she said. "He was fooling around but when my mom found out, he wouldn't leave the woman and we came to live here. I was so young. My mom never said a lot about him after we left. 'There isn't much to say,' she told me once."

She said her dad found someone else when it finally sank in that Claire's mother wouldn't be the trophy wife he could show off to his company buddies.

"Once she figured out she wanted to paint," said Claire, "that was the end of that. Mom never does anything halfway, and once she set her mind to it, even if it was something different than what people expected . . . well, we never see him anymore, anyhow."

"She and my dad got along pretty well, didn't they?" I said. I was drawing on my kid memories of how they would send me away when they were talking, or the times my dad would be in her studio for hours on end, and my mom would have to send me to go get him for supper.

"I guess," said Claire. "Although they were really different in some ways."

"Different how?" Here was some fresh stuff.

"Well, I could hear them talking sometimes when they didn't know I was around. She was always kidding him about his 'it can wait' attitude.

"Oh yeah," I said, "I remember: 'Is the house burning down? Is someone bleeding to death? Is there a tornado?' My mother kids me that I think like that now."

"Even though your dad wasn't a lot like my mom," said Claire, "I think she liked him anyway. It was kind of like she saw there was another way to be happy."

We were both quiet for a while. I suddenly realized it had gotten darker when I couldn't see the edge of the clearing.

Claire broke the silence. "Sometimes I feel it's silly to get so intense about this little piece of land, when the whole planet's really just a little piece of land. I mean, that's space out there," she said, looking up. "Do you realize that? I mean we're on the edge here, looking out like we're on a spaceship."

And as I looked overhead, high up as we were on the wagon, I felt suddenly dizzy like you do at the top of a Ferris wheel when they stop it and the car rocks back and forth? I put out my hand to steady myself and found that it rested on Claire's thigh.

I could see her smile in the dimming light. She leaned her head on my shoulder, then tilted it up in the way that told me I should put my lips to hers.

When I did, Emily guiltily crossed my mind, but then there was something else:

With Emily, yes it could be this same sky with all these wonderful things in it, and I'd feel myself rising to it, but then I would reach . . . it was like a clear glass roof that I could see through but couldn't get past. I never really got *out.* But with Claire—it was like she said, it was more like I was on the edge of something and there was nothing in the way. And falling off, I felt myself *go.* All those years of sadness, wanting, and being alone, melting and flowing out my mouth. I wanted to tell her all this, but instead I said:

"I never thought about it this way. The sky."

"Be quiet," said Claire.

15

FIFTEEN

"Know how to drive a forklift?" Spiro asks me one morning. Vinnie has called in sick, and Lou with his bad eyesight can't be trusted driving anything (EXCEPT FOR A CAR!) and someone needs to move the heavy stuff around.

Even though I never even *sat* in one, if Vinnie could drive it how hard could it be? So I say "Sure, no problem" and as soon as Spiro goes, I have Lou show me the controls.

Lucky for me it's as easy as it looks, forklifts being the concept car of the Great Apes Auto Show: steering wheel, accelerator pedal, brake pedal. Two levers: the left moves the forks up and down, the right lets you shift from forward to neutral to reverse.

Soon I was zipping around the warehouse in the thing. You couldn't really go fast, but it seemed like it, zooming ten inches past the stacked up boxes on each side. It had a spin-

120

ning yellow light on top and a beeper to make it hard to run over anyone except maybe for Barney who sometimes fell sound asleep in the middle of an aisle.

After a day or two I even got pretty good at picking pallets of stuff off a stack and racing them out to the dock. You had to be quick, especially if there was a lineup of trucks.

When Vinnie got back and I started picking orders again, Spiro popped his head out of the office and said "What are you doing? I need you on the forklift."

"But I thought Vinnie . . ." I started to say.

"Don't think so much," said Spiro.

I tried to avoid looking at Vinnie, but I could feel his thousand-yard stare of death smoking the hairs off the back of my neck.

When I sat in the forklift after lunch, I felt a squish. Someone had squeezed a clear line of fresh grease under the front edge of the seat. I wiped my pants off with paper towels from the men's room and didn't say anything.

Maybe I should have.

Next day, I'm racing around, loading boxes of toilet bowls, sinks, and other small fixtures. They came in the night before and had all been piled up to the rafters in one of the more wilderness areas of the warehouse, so it was (a) a dangerous deal getting them on the forks and (2) a long trip to the loading dock.

Now there was something Dad told me when he saw me running to get ready for school one morning. "When you're already really late," he said, "you might as well take your

121

time." But I must've forgotten it. That morning, my clock radio had figured into a dream where, even though I pounded it into a heap of busted plastic, it still kept playing and, when I finally realized what was going on, it was much later than it should be. All the guys had gone in and were already at work. Lou told me a truck radioed in that needed to be loaded and where all these fixtures were that needed to be moved. I jumped on the forklift so I could get the light and beeper going in case Spiro happened to come out.

I don't know if I was being careless. Maybe I didn't worry so much about getting the load all the way on the forks and maybe I figured the stuff was well padded in cardboard and foam anyway and maybe I was getting cocky about how good a fork jockey I was, but this one time, as I raced the length of the warehouse with a full load and broke out onto the loading dock, all of a sudden it was like the thing *surged* ahead, even though my foot was off the accelerator pedal and, seeing the edge of the dock flying up, I panicked and hit the brake—hard—and next this whole pallet of toilets goes sliding off the forks, hits the edge of the dock, hangs for the slow-motion time it would take somebody to jump down and shove them back—except we're all standing there like we're floating on a cloud and this is some entertaining show that's happening down below with those savage earthlings—then tips off and lands upside down with a sound like a dump truck spilling a load of dinner plates down a flight of stairs.

Somehow Spiro is out there even before the driver—who was still backing in—jumps down from her rig and he's in such a fuming, foaming, blooming, seething, steaming rage that he's crushing the can of soda in his hand like a marshmallow, so the stuff is boiling out of the top and dripping at his feet in a puddle that looks like bubbling blood.

"-ack, -ack, -ack, Thackeray!" He can hardly speak. Then, he gets his voice and bellows: "Thackeray! Clean up that mess, punch out, and pick up your pay! You're outta here!"

And then he's gone.

And so am I.

Everybody avoids me like I was radioactive, except for Vinnie, who can't resist a final "Rough luck, Richie," as the clock chomps a notch in my card for the last printed time. Even Claire doesn't come out, although I'm sure she doesn't know—Spiro with soda dripping down his arm is a nearly everyday sight—and I don't want to go in there and drag her down with me in this. I can always call her later.

Even though Mom isn't home yet, I don't feel I can go there. It would remind me too much of my failure—check—my *failures:* the clock ticking in the quiet where I wasn't supposed to be for another six or seven hours, my dad's picture looking down on me from the bookcase. I thought of calling Emily, but felt I needed time to think about how I'd explain to her how I'd lost the job that was supposed to be showing how serious I was.

So in the aimless, too-bright-to-be-out-in-it midmorning, for no particular reason, I find myself driving toward the Harding Estate.

I park across from the entrance, just to think for a few

123

minutes. Right away I notice there's a rent-a-cop car parked inside the gates and a guy eating a sandwich sitting in it.

While I'm there, an OK company truck pulls up to the entrance. The guy gets out of the car and hauls back the gates. He says something to the driver and they both laugh, then stands back as the truck slides on in.

As it disappears into the estate, the guy closes the gates and gives me a long look before stepping back into the car to finish his lunch.

16

Sixteen

When I give Mom the short version of my "What I Did (to Get Fired) This Summer" story, she doesn't look surprised at all. She only says quietly, "Well, there's always *next* summer, I guess." Then she doesn't say anything else.

I don't know how she could have treated me worse.

I ducked Emily, afraid she would be all too eager to get me started filling out business school applications. No sense in piling too much suffering on myself all in one day.

So I found myself laying the whole situation on Claire, half afraid to see how she'd take it. Her mouth dropped open when I got to the edge-of-the-loading-dock part and she got red-faced angry when I got to the Spiro part.

"It's lucky you didn't get killed," she said, her eyes flaring. "The whole *thing* could've gone over and landed on you. It's

125

just like Spiro to blame *you.* The idiot!" And the hug she gave me was followed by a kiss that made it all seem worthwhile.

As I've said, with Claire, *everything* was so much easier. I didn't feel like I had to defend my whole existence every time I spoke. Even though I'd blown it once again, it didn't seem as much "Me Against the World" as it usually did.

"Well, try to look at it positively," Claire said. We sat beside each other in a booth at the Cup'n Spoon, where we met in the sleepy late afternoon after work—Claire's, that is.

"OK," I said. "I've given my mom one more reason to doubt me, I'm not even gonna *try* to get a job for the couple of weeks before school, I'm cash poor, my incomplete isn't done and I'll have to repeat a class now in the fall, I haven't even *begun* to apply for college, and I have no idea what I would study if I did."

"What incomplete?" she said, ignoring my venting.

"You heard of Mr. Bhandaru, the film teacher at my school?" Claire had gone to another school, but I was sure she did. On top of the TV show, he always kicked off the school year with his (take a deep breath) International Global World Premiere Debut Film Festival, where he showed the best movies made in his class the year before.

Did I tell you this was a big production?

He sent out invitations to nearly everyone in town, got the AV people to run oceans of wire around continents of equipment in the auditorium—projectors, screens, sound boards, speakers, lights, live cameras trained on the crowd, you name it—rented a popcorn machine and one of those spotlights you could use to light up Mars if you needed to, and had that roaring away in front of the school as soon as it was halfway dark.

He wore a tux to classes all day and everybody came, even some past grads whose movies were going to be shown.

"The 'Movie Maniac'?" Claire said.

"Maniac is right," I said. "I *wanted* him to flunk me so I wouldn't have to deal with it, but instead he said stuff about how he had faith in me, that I could *do* this project we had to do—make a documentary about something—and he gave me an extension over the summer. Somebody else I guess I'll disappoint," I added.

"But I remember your drawings," she said, putting her hand on mine. "I know Mom was coaching you. She gave up on me. Gram hooked me on horses and I lost interest in everything else—and Mom doesn't waste her time. But I was just talking with her the other day and she said *you* had it—an eye for things."

"You remember those?" I said. "My *drawings*?"

"They were good," she said. I looked at her to make sure she wasn't kidding. She was no-smile serious, all right, although *her* serious somehow took me in, in a way that Emily's didn't.

"But what's drawing got to do with making a film?" I said. "I mean I can draw storyboards but . . ."

Claire slid a little closer as if she was going to tell me a secret. I put my arm around her. "I used to watch old movies on TV with my mom all the time," she said. "Mom would say 'Look at the way that actress has that pointed shadow coming at her. She's going to get stabbed,' or 'See how she's always *above* him—on the stairs or a balcony or something. That shows he's got to come *up* to her level from where he is.' And sometimes she'd even leave the sound off. She said that making a movie is *all* about how you see things."

"Yeah," I said, "I remember Bhandaru used to talk about the *evidence* for things. That you had to *show* the audience, but . . . well, I mostly quit drawing things a long time ago, anyway," I said. "After we left the estate, it was like everything I saw was made in a factory, and there didn't seem any point in it."

I *didn't* say that this was after my dad died and I had stopped really looking and saw no point in *anything*.

"You haven't done *any*?"

"A few."

I told her that when something especially hit me—a thundercloud, its top in bright sunlight, its bottom all purplish and dark, or a jumble of logs, white from a light snow, lying on the brown ground—I'd still take like a *mental* picture and sometimes sketch it out, maybe even splashing on watercolors from an old paint set.

"I'd like to see them," she said, turning her head to me as she leaned back in the bend of my arm.

Since I had nothing to do anyway and was looking for any excuse I could find to keep meeting with Claire, next day I rounded up all my drawings, old and new, and jammed them in a department store dress box Mom had in her closet. I folded up a few storyboards in it too.

Later in the quiet afternoon at the Cup'n Spoon, I laid the box down on the Formica, the late sun squeezing through the window blind, spreading buttery bars across its lid.

Claire quickly picked it up and swiped the table underneath with her hand.

"You should be more careful with these," she said, as I slid in next to her.

She opened the box and began carefully turning pages, looking at the drawings, stopping to read the things I'd written down under them, mostly when I was a kid and my dad was still alive and I was still paying attention. I read over her shoulder:

[*A drawing of my dad with a yellow line on his cheek.*]

"Dad with pollen on his face after he smelled a hosta flower."

and,

[*A drawing of an Osage orange bush.*]

"I asked Dad what Osage oranges were used for, and he said 'Nothing.'

So I asked, 'Then why do we grow them?'

He said, 'It's important to have some things that aren't used for anything.' "

She paused for a longer time at each of the other drawings, which I think you'll get from the things I wrote underneath:

This is some tall, bent grass which is straightening up as the

129

sun dries it out. Each stalk has its own little stream of steam coming off the top of it like a skinny smokestack. All of these streams come together into a cloud that hangs over the field.

And:

Here's a rotten stump behind our cottage. It's covered with bright red fungus and has black and yellow butterflies all over it. Mom thinks it looks ugly and pretty at the same time. "Like a cute girl with a black eye," she says.

And:

This is a catalpa tree which was in the middle of blooming, when it got knocked halfway over in a storm yesterday. It's leaning in the fork of a maple tree next to it. Its flowers look like the smoke shooting out the end of a cannon.

And:

This is a picture of the girl who lives here. She is way up high on horseback and the little sparkles all around her are the sun shining through a million holes in the trees behind her.

"I remember this," she said.

I smiled. We locked eyes for a second.

When she got to the storyboards, I described what was happening in them and said how Bhandaru had vetoed them.

"But you really have something going here," she said, "whether *anybody* agrees with you or not. Have you shown them to anyone?"

"Besides Bhandaru and you?" I said. "Who else would be interested?" I didn't want to bring up Emily and my failed attempts to get her involved.

Claire put her arm through mine. "Maybe *that's* what you

could study in school—art and design—even film." She sounded suddenly excited.

"I thought of that already," I said, "but I'm working on getting away from being so dreamy. You know, giving up on kid ideas."

"I don't think that's such a kid idea." She curled her arm more tightly around mine. I could feel her breast leaning against me. I took a quick glance to see if anyone was looking but, aside from two people with their backs to us at the counter and Jake cleaning out the coffee machine, the place was empty.

"And it's probably something I wasn't meant to be," I said, remembering Emily's comments. "It's more for people who have money and connections. Besides, do you know how many companies hire artists?"

"But, Neal," she said, "if this is what you *want* . . . it could be a *real* possibility. Lots of times people take other jobs if that's what they want to do. My mom always says you should try to live your dreams."

"That's all it is, though," I said. "Just a dream. You can dream all you want, but it's what you *do* that counts."

"Whoever said that?" said Claire. "Dreams are great; they help people get to the place where they *can* do things."

"Oh," I said.

"And my mom, she says that no dream is *just* a dream. Especially if you work to make it come true."

I suddenly had the feeling like someone stuck an ice cube down my shirt.

"Oh!" I repeated.

"And this is all so . . . beautiful," she said, paging through the drawings with her free hand. "It would be a shame. . . ."

"Well," I said. "The subjects made it easy." I stopped her at the drawing of the girl on horseback.

She blushed. "You know what I mean," she said, leaning her head on my shoulder. And as she continued flipping through the drawings, something seemed to occur to her and she sat up straight.

"What kills me," she said, "is I *know* these places—these trees and paths and hanging vines. Here's the way the old horse barn used to look."

"I did most of them on the estate, and from things I remembered there."

"And all of it will be lost," she said. I was afraid she was going to start bawling. "It's too bad. It's too bad," she kept repeating. "I mean it's bad for my mom and me and all, but if everyone could see how beautiful it looks . . . Do you mind if I show these to my mom?"

"Sure, go ahead." I wouldn't mind moving up a notch or two in that woman's opinion.

When Claire finally put away my drawings, the light from the sun was nearly out.

Jake rattled dishes as he stacked them, then reached under the counter.

The diner's bright overhead lights flashed on and everything—the shiny black surface of the table, the chrome-topped salt and pepper shakers, the chipped cups and saucers and scratched spoons, the box of drawings, the gleaming brown rows of Claire's hair up next to my cheek—everything—all lit up. Suddenly it all seemed so sharp and clear and *different*—as if I had just landed from some long trip in space and hadn't really seen anything on this, my home world, for years and years.

17

SEVENTEEN

To give her credit, it was Emily who finally put me over the top (or made me hit bottom) and got me to actually *do* something.

I won't say I was *avoiding* her after I got fired, but I wasn't exactly going out of my way to see her, either. And all this made me feel . . . well, bad—guilty, I guess—owing her so much and everything and my seeing more of Claire on top of it. But I knew that when I saw her I would have to explain everything and that would be so hard, that it was easier to duck her.

I tried to lay low during normal work hours, but one day I had to sneak out to get some groceries for dinner. I drove through back streets—even went to an out-of-the-way store I almost never go to.

I know you're really going to think that I'm one oar short

of a full deck, but I really *like* going to the supermarket. I mean there's all this stuff: bread and eggs and antifreeze and birthday candles and salami and shoelaces and dental floss and plastic snow shovels and baby buttwipes—all jammed in there under lights bright enough for a helicopter landing pad—with people pushing these wheelbarrow carts around, squinting and squeezing and sniffing at it all. Just the bizarre packages and signs alone make me laugh.

Beats daytime TV any day.

And so here I am dodging down an aisle, a bag of noodles under my arm like a football, sidestepping carts—don't have enough for a cart myself, and I'm *not* carrying one of those fruity-looking baskets—having a good old time gaping at the goofy boxes ("New Low-Fat Ravioli Flakes! Now With Pork Chop Flavor!") when, as I'm cutting through the frozen food section, who do I run into just as she turns the corner, but Emily!

I *knew* I was had, right away, so before she can even say "Neal!" I'm gibbering out the whole OK Construction and Supply Company Forklift Toilet Disaster in three-part harmony with backup on squeaky cart wheels getting it out and over with.

Emily says nothing at first. As meaningful as my mother's nothing, but with a slightly different feel to it.

"Oh, Neal," she finally says, hugging me right in the middle of the supermarket aisle. She doesn't let go until some lady comes tugboating along pushing a barge of food and glares at us like Hey, how about taking your puppy love to the dog food aisle?

But the next thing Emily says is, "How are you *ever* going to get good references?" like it was my fault.

"I *told* you they had it out for me. That Cooney guy? Remember? I'm sure he was ratting on me and I bet it was Vinnie put the grease on the seat and messed with the pedal on the forklift and . . ."

"Now, Neal," she says, giving me the serious eyebrows look.

"Look," I say, trying to wriggle free, "I've got a few more things to buy and I've got to be back home before Mom gets . . . I'm supposed to do supper tonight. Can we meet later? I'll give you a call?"

"Neal, I've got a couple of meetings coming up and I've got a pile of applications to go through. . . ."

"But I want to talk to you about some ideas that—"

"I need to get moving here," she says, looking at her list. "What if I call you when things aren't so crazy?" As she pecks me on the cheek I get a glimpse of her face as she pulls away. She has that faraway look in her eyes like the one she'd had when we were back in the shed—like she was looking somewhere past me.

After she leaves, I see myself standing there, reflected in the glass door of a freezer, looking as cold as the boxes of frozen pizza inside. For some reason, though, right after this, as I'm walking up to the checkout, I remember back in third grade when Presley Kulaki would jack me up for my lunch every day. "Better hand it over, Mighty Mouse," he'd say, his fat hairy knuckles lined up with my nose. It was very satisfying when, one day on my way to school, I threw out the baloney in my sandwich and swapped it for a gym shoe liner—satisfying, but not so smart. And I had the feeling right now that I was about to do something similar.

After all, what claim did Emily have on me if she was going to give me the cold shoulder? For the time being why not forget about business school and any future that included her and station wagons with downspouts? Why not use the time left of my summer break to do something that made sense to *me?* Why not do something that might work for some future *I* imagined?

When all was said and done, what did I have to lose? Or, to put it another way:

What?

Did I *have* to lose?

Why not use the remaining time I had this summer to at least salvage something from this wreck and do a really good job—serious for once in my life—on the documentary for Bhandaru?

It was Claire telling me that everything on the estate would be lost that gave me my subject:

The documentary I would make would be about the estate.

Bhandaru was teaching summer school and told me to call when I had an idea. When I did and explained to him why

137

it was important to me to make this film; that it was the last place on earth with some link to my dad's memory, he said, "Finally, getting out from behind your hands. Go ahead."

I asked him if he had any suggestions.

"Look for the ghost in the viewfinder," he said, whipping his cape around in front of his face (I imagined) and before I could ask what he meant, he hung up.

Thanks for the big help, Mr. B.

So I dug out our ancient vacationland video camera. It was so big that all our home shots—almost none of Dad since he was mostly taking them—were on a slant from it tilting him sideways. But it would do.

I looked through my notes from the film class for advice Bhandaru had given about documentaries: how the best modern ones tried to stay out of the way of their subjects; how they tried to show life as it really was, like you were looking through a pane of glass instead of a camera lens.

Of course, he said, you had to be prepared—that was the point of the storyboards—but then I already knew a lot about Claire and her mom and the house and land they lived on.

Remembering Bhandaru's emphasis on the facts of the situation, I thought at the very least, it might be healthy for me to get a good look at things as they *really* were instead of how I *remembered* or *imagined* or *wished* or *dreamed* them to be.

I thought How hard could it be, anyway? I mean did you ever notice what happens when you point a camera at people? They can't *help* doing stuff. That takes care of actors.

138

As for scripts, you don't need them either, since people just talk. There's no retakes or anything since they can't screw up their lines, and the scenery is whatever is behind them. What could be simpler?

When I told Claire about my idea, she was enthusiastic. "Great," she said, all warm next to me in the diner. "And I could give a tour—like narrate it if you want."

I warned her that I didn't entirely know what I was doing.

"You have a wonderful way of seeing things," she said, taking my hand and looking me straight in the eye. "I know you'll do great."

So why not?

18

EIGHTEEN

"Where are you off to?"

Mom surprises me. She's usually not up so early on Saturday. Neither am I—or any other day, for that matter. Since I'm not working I've been using up lots of my Unemployment Land tickets riding the Big Comfy Bed.

"You're up early," I say.

She smiles. "Couldn't sleep so good," she says.

"I'm supposed to meet Claire out on the estate," I tell her.

She stops smiling. With no makeup and a bedhead, it suddenly hits me she's older than I always think of her.

"You're going out *there* again?"

"I'm going to do my movie," I say. "You know, from the incomplete?"

She's all of a sudden quiet. I hear her slippers shuffling on the linoleum.

"What's the matter?" I say.

"Nothing," she says, "nothing. I just wish you wouldn't make a habit of it, going out there."

"Mom," I say. "It's not like it's heroin or picking my nose or something. I have to do this thing by the end of the summer and it seemed like a good idea."

"OK," she says, softening a little. "But Neal, honey, it's just that I worry about you living in the past. You're so young and you've got—"

"Don't worry so much, Mom," I say. I let her give me another hug—it makes her feel better—and I let it drop.

In another hour I'm following Claire's beat old pickup into the estate once again—she's let me in the back entrance, avoiding the leased police. This time I have my camera and tape and other stuff bouncing on the car seat beside me.

If I thought she and her mom were going to make some kind of preparations—like they would have everything all set up, or would specially dress for my mega-production—I soon found I was wrong.

The moment I got out of my car, while the blue smoke from Claire's pickup still hung in the air, I switched on the camera and started shooting.

Although we weren't using a script, we worked out some

141

things Claire would say and I had drawn some storyboards based on what I knew and what she told me to expect.

CLOSE-UP: CLAIRE TALKS into the camera, which gradually zooms out to show the house rising up behind her.

"Well here we are on the formerly fabulous Harding Estate," she says, "now home to the formerly rich and famous Harding women.

"You might not expect it," she says—the frame expands to include more and more of the house—"stuck as it is in the middle of an ordinary suburb out here, but the property has an interesting story to tell.

"My great-grandfather Barnabas Harding first got this land over a hundred years ago as a political favor . . ." and she goes into a short history of the place. As she speaks, I do a slow 360-degree shot of the house and grounds, all lit with the steady glow of the warm light of the late summer sun.

"My grandfather, Thaddeus, who was Barnabas's only son, inherited it and he never set foot on it either, until he decided one day, after a business deal went bad, to come out to the Midwest here and become what my mom calls a miner. What he was digging for, she says, was a rich vein of people dumb enough to give him money. And here in town he hit the mother lode.

"He started a business making spark plugs—this was when cars

first got popular—and as the money piled up, he built the main house and the garden and laid out the horse trails."

Zoom in to a medium shot and then pan the crumbling, overgrown garden wall.

"Then he married my grandmother, who was born around here and who he'd hired to care for the horses.

"He lost nearly all of his money during the Depression, and died soon after that, but by then he had stashed away some in a trust fund. This paid out just enough for my grandmother to keep things up.

"But my grandfather loved the place so much that he wanted to keep it exactly as it was, forever."

Close with a long shot: the meadow to one side of the house falling off to a wooded area, the trees all sparkling in the light.

"So he wrote in his will that the trust fund money would continue to flow only if the place was kept in one whole piece. Once the first square foot of it was sold off, it would all go to charity.

"My grandmother tried to get it changed, but the trustees wouldn't budge and now it's love it or lose it, as my mother says."

Close-up on Claire: "Let's take a walk around the grounds and see how things look today."

A point of view shot—like we're looking through her eyes as Claire walks through the gardens. You can hear twigs crunching underfoot and the swish of shrubs as she brushes past.

143

Close-up inserts:

The vine-blurred posts of a fence with only a few of its rails still attached, the scrub and long grass on one side looking like the scrub and long grass on the other.

Tree roots that have grown around and through the stones of the walkway, jumbling them so much in some places that the walk disappears.

Medium shot: an old wooden arched door with fancy lock and iron hinges set in a brick wall. It's nearly hidden by shrubs, which have shot out long sucker branches that droop to the ground, sprouting whole other new worlds of bushes.

"This is the entrance to the garden," says Claire, walking into the frame then parting the shrubs so she can get close to the door.

"My grandmother locked the garden years ago to keep out deer and rabbits and then she lost the key. Mom and I finally found it in the false bottom of one of Gram's old jewelry boxes."

Extreme close-up: A big, rusty old-fashioned skeleton key going in the door's lock. A hand and then a pair of hands forcing and finally turning it.

Over Claire's shoulder: Claire shoving the door, which won't budge. The cameraman's foot sticks into the frame and kicks the door and it finally gives.

Close-up: The door fights her all the way as she pushes it into the ropy vines and small trees that have grown up blocking the way.

"Well, as you can see," Claire says, the camera whirring as she speaks, "if you like your gardens wild and natural, this is the place."

A slow pan around the inside of the garden.

"There's so much stuff," Claire says out of the frame, "you can hardly see where the walls are."

Medium shot: a huge apple tree that overarches the whole garden. Claire walks into the frame and picks up something and holds it out.

"Looks like they're wormy," she says.

Extreme close-up: A mangled little green fruit with black spots held in the palm of a hand.

"This tree hasn't been pruned or sprayed in years; it's gotten out of hand. If these things fell on you from up there, they'd kill you."

Point of view: Claire as she walks the remains of the garden path.

"Underneath all that growth, in the middle over there," she says, "is a fountain."

Close-up: A pair of hands parting a mass of weeds. You can barely see the edge and faded blue bottom of the pool of a fountain, now chipped and crisscrossed with thousands of cracks.

"Used to be a statue out there in the center," she says.

I forgot what I was doing and put the camera down from my eye. Only remembering then to turn it off.

It took me a minute to get used to seeing without looking through the viewfinder. Everything seemed much less colorful in real life—like the street outside when you walk out of a movie.

"Where is it?" I said. "The statue."

"I remember asking Grams about it once," said Claire, "and she said your dad fixed it, but didn't connect it so good or something and when the pool froze solid one winter, it fell over and we had to take it out."

"What happened to it?" I asked.

"I don't know," she said. "That was years ago—not long after you left . . . but I know we didn't get rid of it, so it would have to be . . . Wait!" she said, suddenly thinking of something. "Follow me."

Turning the camera back on, I followed her in the viewfinder with one eye, keeping the other open so I didn't fall in a hole.

POINT OF VIEW: Claire pushes through the tall grass and weeds, following a path so nearly gone in all this overgrowth you would have to know it was there to begin with. She soon comes up on a gray shed next to the garden wall. It's made up to look like a house, with a window and a flower box and all. She pulls open its door against the high grass that grows right up to it and goes in.

Close-up: the shed's open doorway. It's too dark for the camera to record anything inside, but you hear Claire, her voice muffled, say: "Yes, here it is."

Zoom out to medium shot: Claire backs out of the shed and moves out of the frame. The dark space inside the doorway is suddenly harshly lit by the camera's built-in light. There's a moment of red as the light saturates the scene, then the camera adjusts and we see coming into focus the face—in stone—of a little boy. The camera focuses and follows the ripples of stone behind him—more brightly lit by a square of light that comes in through the window of the shed. The shapes form themselves into the robes and then the dreamy face of an angel looking down at the little boy.

"Yes, that's it," Claire says from out of the frame. "The statue that used to be in the fountain. Grams called it 'Whizzer and Watcher.' "

19

NINETEEN

OVER THE SHOULDER: Claire walks up the slanty front steps of the Big House. The scene gets jumpy as the camera follows her on the rough stairs.

Close-up: the double front doors of the house. The screening flaps loose on one side as she opens it and Claire has to bear down with both hands to release the dull brass latch. The door squawks like a cat caught in a vacuum cleaner hose.

Inside it's so dark, you can barely see Claire standing in the front hall. She tries a light switch but nothing happens and she shrugs. The camera light comes on, making her squint and put her hand in front of her eyes, so I turn it off.

"Wait," she says. The camera follows her as she opens the front door to let in the light.

"As you might guess, the estate house didn't always look like this," she says as I pan slowly across the peeling wallpaper, the cobwebbed railing to the grand entry staircase, the hole in the plaster on the landing.

"But the cost of keeping up such a big place ate up the trust fund, and little by little we had to just let things go."

Point of view: Claire walks into a room with empty bookcases that stretch all the way to the ceiling. She stands in front of one.

Medium shot: "We sold off almost all the books and furniture and other things," she's saying, "but after a while, there just wasn't much left. We kept this." She points to the wall over the blackened fireplace.

Next in extreme close-up you see a painting of some old guy with a whiskbroom beard and a funny look on his face like he had a mouthful of live sandworms.

"This is my grandfather, Thaddeus Harding, who owned the sparkplug factory? He's one of the ghosts that haunts this place."

"Ghosts?" says a voice from out of the frame. Bhandaru says you're not supposed to talk off-camera, but I can't help getting into it.

"Grams—my grandmother—always said that ghosts have to be wished by somebody. She said that the only ghosts are those that we want to be here. So somebody must want him around—probably someone he owed money to."

Maybe this was it. I'd have to concentrate on wishing back some vision of my dad. See-through or not I'd take him.

We went on for a while like this, Claire giving a travelogue as we walked through the place, me following her with the camera. Wires stuck out of the ceiling where the light fixtures were sold off and there were no lamps, so I had to use the camera light, which made it look like—did you ever watch one of those TV shows where they dive to the bottom of the ocean where it's pitch dark and all you can see is where the spotlight shines?

POINT OF VIEW shot: Every once in a while a clock or a chair that's covered up with a sheet, or a bureau as big as a sunken ship suddenly floats into the frame. Paintings leaning against the walls down at floor level swim into the frame like schools of tropical fish.

"They're all Mom's," says Claire, from outside the frame. "Can you believe we're running out of room for them?"

Finally through the viewfinder I see the long hallway with the brightly lit doors at the end.

"Let me go ahead," she says, "so my mother knows we're coming."

Close-up: the closed doors with the light pouring in through their many panes.

"OK," she says, poking her head out like her mother had the other day. "You can come in now."

Point of view: The room through the doors is flooded in sunlight. Windows run the whole length of one wall, letting in a steady light so strong that again it takes the camera a few seconds to adjust.

Into the frame drift easel after easel—an army of them—each with a brightly colored painting propped on it. The camera hangs on each one before it moves on:

Fruit in a bowl on a table. One orange is cut open and has what looks like a computer board inside.

People riding department store escalators that join one to the other in a square so you can't figure out if they're going up or down.

A giant apple in a rowboat in a living room.

A tiny girl holding the string of a kite except she's the one up in the air at the end of the string.

Point of view shot, close-up: The floor is totally covered with scraps of paper, old brushes and cans, empty tubes of paint, and old pieces of canvas and frame. There's a shuffling, crunching, snapping sound underfoot as all this stuff gets stepped on. The image in the camera jiggles like out on the steps.

The camera tilts up from the floor into a medium shot:

On a stool by the easel nearest the windows sits a woman dressed in a gray sweatshirt with a school name on it, tight black pants that come halfway up her shins, black half boots with heels,

151

her brown hair bunched roughly out of the way in a vegetable store rubber band like Claire's.

"Just a moment," the woman says.

Close-up, over the woman's shoulder: The frame is filled with a confused mess of swirling colors, yellows and blues and purples, lines and ridges of paint. As the camera zooms out, the shadows and lines begin to blend, then turn into an image: an old wagon piled high with merry-go-round horses—paint fading, legs missing, manes chipped. There's a man hitched to it, straining as he pulls the whole thing. Claire's mom is dabbing at the man's shirt, making it look all dirty and torn.

"There." As the camera zooms out farther, the woman's head and shoulders come into the frame. "That's a good break point," she says.

She's not completely in focus and I step back even more, getting her more fully into the frame as she wipes her brush on a rag and dunks it into a paint-smeared can.

Close-up: The can sits on a Formica kitchen table covered with a dozen other such cans—fat and short and thin and tall and everything in between—each with one or ten paint-blackened brush handles sticking out of it, so the tabletop looks like what's left after a forest fire.

"So, you want to make a movie of the old place?" says Claire's mother out of the frame.

152

"I'd like to get some record of it, especially since Claire says you might lose it," I say.

"I told Neal how we can't afford to keep everything going," Claire says.

Medium shot: Claire's mother in front of the painting she's working on.

"You know what would be the only thing I'd miss if it came to that?" she says. "The way things look when I look out." She flicks her hand at the windows.

"What do you mean?" I say. I'm nearly afraid of her she's so stunning, but I feel safe behind the camera.

"Have you ever slept outdoors for a couple of days?" she says.

The frame moves up and down as I nod. "I used to camp out behind the cottage for weeks in the summers."

"You can live almost anywhere with a tent, a sleeping bag, and some matches," she says. "But once you pick the spot, you define your space. You become tied to *this* piece of ground," she says, pointing to the room around her as she talks, "*these* surroundings. And your tent flaps become a frame for looking at things. You get a point of view. Do you see?"

"Yes," I say. I'm not sure I do.

"So when it comes right down to it," she says, "it's not so much the house, but the way it helps everything *else* make sense—the wonderful way it sets off things and gives you a particular way to see the world."

153

"So, Mom," says Claire from off camera, sensing I'm lost, "tell Neal about your pictures."

"What's to tell?" she says. "I try to say everything I have to say in painting them."

"Maybe you could tell Neal how you got started," Claire says.

She considers. "Well, you become an artist when you start looking at things and I don't know if there was a time when I wasn't," she says. "At first I thought there was something wrong with me. People were always saying, 'Look at the red leaves,' and I was saying 'Where?' 'Cause I always saw *all* the colors. The oranges . . . and yellows . . . and umbers . . ."—she held up tubes of paint—"and crimsons . . . and mauves that were their *real* colors. I didn't know from 'red.' Kids do that, you know—they see all the colors in something, then after a while they learn not to."

"They learn to *not* see?" says the Voice from Nowhere.

"To not trust their own eyes," she says. "Instead they start seeing things in ways other people want them to. Look at this painting, for instance."

I zoom in to where it fills the frame.

"People think that a person's flesh is one color," she says. "But get in close on the face here."

I zoom in to an extreme close-up.

"See? It's made up of reds and yellows and blues and soft purples—a lot of different shades that blend into what we call the 'color' of someone's skin."

154

As I shoot, I can see out of the corner of my eye that Claire is wandering down the row of windows and looking out.

Close-up on Claire's mother: "Did you ever see those puzzles in kids' books where you're supposed to find the five animals in a tree—a cat, a dog, a bird, a duck, a bear? Well, I never could. And then when somebody else would show me, I'd see they weren't really animals at all, but just some lines that you were supposed to see were a rabbit or something. Luckily I was stubborn; I've worked my whole life against the way people tried to make me see. It didn't always make me popular."

This is starting to sound familiar all of a sudden. "How so?" I say.

"Seeing things differently," she says, "makes people suspicious. They put you in with those who have visions and hear voices. They think you're weird or strange. You get real isolated, and then you start to see things different all the more. It wasn't until I studied art in college that I realized this wasn't a bad place to be."

"My father always talked a lot about seeing," I say.

"Yes," says Claire's mother, pausing before she went on. "He told me once that truly seeing things was his little secret to keep from going crazy; his way of keeping things fresh and new. He used to say that spring never comes again . . ."

" 'It's a new one each time.' Right?" I say.

"Right," she says. "If you only just open your eyes."

I suddenly feel dizzy and put down the camera and sit on a stool. My memories of my father were so strange that I'd been starting to think I was making *him* up. To hear somebody repeat something he said, especially in that place where he'd spent so much time . . .

"Are you all right?" says Claire's mother.

Claire looks back from where she stands in the light at the windows.

"Neal?" she says.

"I'll be OK," I say. "Guess I should've had breakfast."

"Let me go get something for you," Claire says.

Her mother watches me from her stool. She looks like she's thinking about something.

Claire comes back with a glass of orange juice and a plate with a couple of pieces of brown bread on it. "This was the quickest I could find. Here," she says, shoving cans and brushes and paint tubes aside to make room on a table.

I pick up a piece of bread and notice the little flecks of bran in it.

Her mother speaks. "I think in many ways we were the same, your father and I. He wasn't an artist, but he *did* have his own, stubborn, one-of-a-kind way of looking at things. I think that's partly why he had a hard time getting along with people."

I don't know what to say. I take a drink of juice. I notice the little bubbles on the top where the juice meets the glass.

Claire's mom continues to watch me closely; then she seems to make a decision.

"Come over here," she says, standing. "I want to show you something."

Still wobbly, I pick up the camera and follow her through the easel forest to the far wall of the studio where the sunlight doesn't reach. In the dimness I can make out a paint-spattered dropcloth covering something on the floor that's two or three feet high and runs the whole length of the wall.

Claire's mother begins rolling back the cloth, uncovering an unframed painting leaning against the wall.

It's of a naked man carrying a little naked boy in his arms as they fly off the edge of a cliff.

The man has a huge set of golden wings sprouting from his back.

I feel a chill ripple through me.

You know how there are people in some countries who don't want their picture taken, like they say you're stealing their soul or something?

That's how I felt.

"You can't *do* that," is the first thing that comes out of my mouth. "That's *mine.*"

Claire's mother doesn't answer, but rolls back the canvas to show a second painting: the same man—my father; it *has* to be—striding through the woods on a tremendously long pair of legs.

And a third: he's standing over the gate to a garden wall, his body and legs blending into the wall itself. He has a wreath of colorful leaves on his head.

And a fourth: he's sitting in a broad field, tiny next to a giant tree, both him and the tree all to one side of the picture and nothing but all meadow in between until you get to the other side where there's a bull facing him.

And a fifth: he's made of stone standing in a fountain, his hands on the shoulders of a little stone boy in front of him, steadying him while the boy takes a pee.

And on and on until all the paintings are uncovered—maybe ten in all, each having a man at the center of them that I couldn't see as anyone but my father, and most of them the same as my moviedreams.

I feel dizzy and hollow-headed like my brain is being sucked out of my eyeballs. I sit on the floor right on top of all the junk, facing the paintings so I can be closer to them.

"Are you OK?" asks Claire.

"I don't know," I say, putting my hands over my eyes to block out the images for a few seconds. But I can't. They keep whirling in my head like the coming attractions in a movie.

Claire's mother by now has taken the dropcloth completely away and is folding it up. "Here, help me," she says to Claire.

I sit there, still numb, as they work. After they're done with it and dump it in a corner, Claire pushes some of the wreckage aside and sits down, putting her arm around my shoulder.

"Your father was a great model." Claire's mother is standing above us. She has her arms folded, one hand up to her chin, and she's all wrapped up in studying the paintings.

"I don't just look at the body, you know," she says. "There has to be something *there,* otherwise it doesn't work for me. And your father had it. He was a dreamer and dreamers do the heavy lifting, and it gives them . . . well . . . definition, I guess. Like body builders in a way."

She stands before the painting where my dad is saving me with the wings. "And they can't always be counted on to do the practical things like hooking the door to the guard dogs' kennel."

She begins walking along the length of the paintings, talking to them instead of Claire and me.

"So sometimes they grow wings and long legs or get a distant stare, and they're not always there when you need them."

She suddenly seems to remember us sitting there.

"You used to come in here with him when he sat for me—you were very little—and I'd give you my props to play with—some plastic fruit or something—and you'd sit in front of these paintings for hours and hours."

"I didn't remember," I say.

"Well, Mother didn't want you in the house here when you were older and when all of you left after Mother intruded . . ."

I'm afraid to ask Intruded in what? but she must read the question in my face, so she stops and explains.

"She came out to the garden one day when your dad was modeling for that painting there." She points to the one where he looks like the statue. "I'd been working with him

159

nude and . . . well, she drew all the wrong conclusions and flew out of control as only Mother could. There really wasn't anything else between us. He was married and I wasn't going to cause anyone the kind of grief I'd gone through. Next I knew she's storming over to the cottage, and then, next I knew, all of you were gone. She had hold of the purse strings, so there wasn't much I could do."

Claire touches the back of her hand to my cheek, then stands and walks along the length of the wall, past her mother, looking at the images down the whole row.

"I kept them hidden back here so she wouldn't destroy them," Claire's mother was saying.

The sun has been moving lower in the sky and coming more directly through the studio windows to where it starts to light up the row of paintings.

"*Look* at these, Neal," Claire says.

I don't say anything. I'm not sure if I can handle it.

"They would be *great* for your movie," she says.

With Claire's urging, I pick up the camera and put it to my eye, shooting in extreme close-up like I'd done with the painting Claire's mother was working on.

AT FIRST LIKE before, all you can see are shapes and how the colors swirl together, and then I begin to pull back and you can see the bigger forms that they make up:

My dad sitting like *The Thinker* on a rock shaped like a woman's breast;

My dad looking up amazed at a sky whose blue flows like a stream through islands of clouds. Leaping down out of the watery blue is a trout;

My dad crossing a stream on a bridge that isn't there;

My dad in a dark kitchen at night with the refrigerator door open, his arm shielding his eyes from the bright rays of light that pour like heaven from inside.

As I shoot, I feel the dizziness and confusion start to dry up and something start to come loose. Something that's been knotted up inside me all these years since Dad died. Something that's been blocking me from doing what I knew I should be at school, that I'd felt climbing up my neck when Spiro stuck me with those dirty jobs, that I felt holding me back from putting my arms around my mother when she hugged me, that I felt was making my mind narrow down like a set of tongs, to hold tight onto the tiny melting piece of memory that was left in my mind of my poor, dead dad, not letting him go to where he needed to go and I needed him to go, and at that instant, I feel it all begin falling away like some heavy wet plaster cast sliding off in big soggy chunks. I feel like the way a snake must feel shucking off its old dead skin and my eyes fill with tears, at first so it's only a thin wet smear between me and the pictures in the viewfinder, but then more and more until all I can see are the glowing mixtures of colors melting one into the other. Even through the blur, I know I'm truly *seeing* again.

"Yes," I say under my breath, as I shoot along the length of these bright, strange, familiar images.

"Yes, yes, yes."

20

Wouldn't you know it? A couple of days later, just as I'm starting to explore some of the other exciting attractions in Unemployment Land: the Tunnel of Total Despair, the Long Boring Afternoon Flume Ride—I get a letter from Spiro, saying my "suspension with pay" (!?) is over since: "our investigation has determined that operator error could not be confirmed as the enabling factor in the incident on said date," and a whole bunch of other legal used bull food all adding up to the fact that they had no evidence to blame me for the forklift accident.

Enclosed was a nice, fat check for back pay.

There was one small hitch: If I signed and deposited it, said the letter, I could never sue OK Construction and Supply in this universe or any other universe known or as yet to be discovered. Spiro signed the letter himself, but I suspect a couple of fat lawyers were sitting on top of him at the time.

I knew there had to be a story to it and next day at the Cup'n Spoon, Jake filled me in: Vinnie was driving the forklift the day after I was "suspended" and he ran it completely off the loading dock and broke his arm. He was suing the place for a couple of million saying there was some kind of defect in the thing. So this was OK Construction's way of covering their broad behinds in case I wanted to get in on the action.

I can't prove it, but I'm still convinced that the real reason I was fired to begin with was that someone—Cooney?—was telling Spiro bad things about me—how I seemed to be much too interested in what was going on at the estate. How maybe I was a spy for another company, or a tree-hugging "Save the Bat Lice" type. (Although there were some foxy maples I would hug long before I would even *touch* certain people.)

Why would someone have it out for me? There's no figuring people. I know a guy at school who likes burnt cookies.

My final guess is that they were just looking for an excuse to get rid of me all along and the forklift tune had a catchy beat they thought they could dance to. But then with Vinnie nearly killing himself and all the tricky legal steps, I guess they decided to sit it out.

See? Just because I'm delirious doesn't mean it wasn't real.

Does it?

But, believe me when I tell you this: No matter *whoever* had been up to *whatever,* and what the real situation was, my only interest was in never seeing the place again. So I endorsed the check and set it, along with Spiro's letter, on the table with the other mail where Mom would be sure to see it.

I wasn't there when she got home, but she never did say much to me about it, except "They really must be worried." She really hadn't said anything much to begin with, so she left it at that. Maybe she was supposed to lie and say "I *knew* you would come through"?

As for Emily, I didn't know *what* I felt. To begin with, there was all I owed her and—let's be honest here—all I *got* from her, and I didn't know whether I was about to give it all up.

Since the day in the supermarket when I told her I lost the job, she stopped calling me back. When I did get her she'd tell me she sent her hair out to the dry cleaners, or she was having a spleen transplant or something, and she just couldn't go anywhere. I translated this as "Get lost."

But I wanted to be sure and kept looking for an opportunity. Finally one late afternoon just before the term started I cornered her.

It was one of those days where you get your schedule and supplies list and books. I was trying to find my new locker when I glanced in a classroom I was walking by.

There was Emily, sitting alone, writing something in a book.

"Hi," I said, stepping halfway into the room.

165

She looked up startled like she was caught going through the files in the principal's office in her underwear.

"Oh," she said.

"Remember me?" I said.

"Neal," she said. "There's going to be a meeting in here in—"

"Nobody's here yet," I said. I stepped all the way in and closed the door.

This made her look even more uncomfortable.

I sat down at a desk beside her. We both faced the front.

I saw the book she was writing in was one of those planner things. You know, where there are little spaces to account for every moment of your life and a little fill-in-the-blank tombstone on the last page?

"How's things?" I said, looking up at the blackboard. "It's been hard to catch up with you."

"There's a *lot* going on with school starting and everything." She held up the book for proof. True to Emilyness, the spaces on the pages she showed me were all filled in and we hadn't even begun classes yet.

"I finished my movie," I said.

"Good," she said. "Great. How did it come out?"

"Good, I think," I said.

"What was it about?"

"The estate," I said. "You know, where we lived when my dad was the caretaker?" I didn't want to get into Claire and her mother so I left it at that.

We both stared ahead for a moment.

"I wonder where everyone is?" Emily said, looking at the closed door.

"I mean, it's not exactly done. I have to edit it yet and show it to Bhandaru. I'd like to get it in the festival," I said.

"I'd like to see it sometime," she said, taking a quick look at her watch.

"Sure," I said. "I'll let you know."

She suddenly stood up. A face had appeared in the small glass panel in the door. It was some YAC guy I'd seen her talking to before—tall, with dark hair and glasses. She opened the door.

"Em, didn't anybody tell you we moved it to the computer lab?" he said.

"OK, Steve," she said, and rushed over and gathered up her things, flinging a " 'Bye" over her shoulder as she went out.

I could hear them fast-talking each other in the hall. I sat there in the empty room for a minute.

One of the teachers, probably Miss Field, who taught literature and wore a beret, had decorated the classroom already. She had written a quote at the top of the board:

"What doesn't kill me makes me stronger."—Nietzsche

I took an eraser and piece of chalk, got rid of "stronger," and, in my best imitation of Miss Field's handwriting, wrote "nauseous."

Bhandaru seemed surprised to see me when I showed up knocking on his office door, hugging three or four tapes in my arms, but he let me get into the labs to edit the things anyway, and I juggled, jiggled, jangled, cut them up, and put them back together every which way I could think of to try to make the thing work.

Like a miracle, it all came together just under the deadline for Bhandaru's big show. He took the tape home with him one night and called me aside in the hall the next day between classes.

"You are to be included," he said, and I almost thought I saw him smile.

Maybe it was just gas.

Well, the night of the International Global World Premier Debut Film Festival came. True to form, Bhandaru wore his tux and hired the popcorn machine and the spotlight.

A good crowd turned out, word of his showmanship having spread far and wide. My mom and Claire came, of course. Claire said she'd tried to get her mother to show, but she wouldn't. I didn't see Emily anywhere.

The other movies weren't bad—funny and interesting:

One of a guy who trains his dog to fish. At the end the dog catches one and drops the pole and jumps in after the fish.

One by some girl of her twin sisters and how they switch places with each other—actually doing it on camera before some big event where an award was given up on a stage, with the other whispering to the camera in the background.

Another about old people at a doughnut shop who keep the place open when the owner gets sick and take turns behind the counter so they don't miss their morning get-together.

After a couple of others, my movie—on the program as "Memory Mansion," a title suggested by Bhandaru himself—was shown: dead last.

Claire looked great on the big projection screen; the garden looked mysterious, the house looked big and gloomy, the land and its features—the Chasm, Snake Creek, and whatever other scenery I could pack in—looked big and broad and majestic.

The scenes in the studio were brilliant with sun—the light blotting everything out until I got the camera adjusted—unintended but not a bad effect.

In fact, my clumsy camera work—a few sky and ground shots, blurred sequences where I forgot to put on the auto focus, some cuts where one person appeared where another had just been standing, the camera nodding up and down with my head, me talking off-camera—it was bad enough overall that it looked like A Statement—like I had *intended* it in some bleeding-edge way.

Claire's mom looked like the artist she was—slightly strange but thoughtful. The paintings—especially those Dad had posed for—came off unique and weird—two things that aren't at all bad to have in a film.

All her comments about seeing and reality and all the other good stuff she'd mentioned that day made for a pretty satisfying script. I intercut her comments about my dad in with close-ups of the main male figure in each of the paintings.

Finally I framed up a couple of stunning views from the door and windows to go with the things she said about the importance of place. At the very end, I used a dim shot of the angel and little boy statue and faded it out with Claire's mother's voice-over, talking about how dreams can get lost if we're not careful, but if we go and look and shine a light, we may still find them hidden away somewhere waiting to be brought back out into daylight. The last words on the sound-track as the screen went to black were the last few lines from a poem that she was quoting:

"Dreams can do what deeds can't dream."

People were mostly quiet while the movie was showing, so I couldn't figure out how they were taking it, but at the end when the lights came up, they applauded wildly and I saw a couple of kids pointing me out. Bhandaru—like he did with everyone—made me get up and take a bow. There was a Q and A session and the first one was from a lady up front:

"Where did you ever find such a wonderful painter?" The question was to me and the crowd mumbled in agreement.

"I didn't find her," I blurted out, "she's her mother," pointing to Claire, who was sitting next to me.

This got an unplanned laugh.

"How long has she been painting?"

I looked toward Claire for the answer. "All her life," Claire said, standing up next to me. "She always felt it as the way to best express herself."

"I love that series with the man," said a young woman, dressed in a business jacket and skirt. "The last ones you showed? Was that her husband in those?"

I avoided looking at my mother and didn't know what to say. Claire finally spoke up. "I don't think that a real person like him exists," she said.

"At least not with the wings," I added.

This got another laugh.

"Does she sell her paintings?" an older man with a crew cut and bow tie asked.

"I don't know," said Claire, who by now had taken over things, taking some of the heat off me. "She had them in a gallery once, but no one seemed interested and she took them out."

Afterward, I was a lobby celebrity. There was a landscaper guy who was impressed that such a big, beautiful piece of undeveloped property still sat in the middle of town. A bunch of people shook my hand, and three or four left their names saying they were interested in buying paintings if they were for sale.

"Do you think your mother would be interested?" I asked Claire as we walked arm in arm out to the parking lot. "In selling them, you know?"

"Could be," she said. "Why are *you* so interested?"

"Because I have an idea," I said.

My mom had been quiet through the whole movie and, when I glanced over at her, she even seemed caught up in it. She took in the whole part with the paintings of Dad without blinking.

Maybe she *didn't* recognize him in the paintings.

Maybe she believed the stuff Claire said at the end about him not being real.

Maybe golden armadillos would start flying out of my nose.

She patted my arm and smiled at me when the lights came up. I could see her eyes were shining, though, so I knew something was up.

"Well, what did you think?" I said when we got home and she put on her bathrobe, made her cup of tea, and sat down at the kitchen table. I stood leaning against the counter, my arms crossed.

"I told you," she said. "I loved it. You did a beautiful job."

"And?" I said.

" 'And?' What?" She wouldn't look at me, but kept stirring the hot water and tea bag in her cup. By now the stuff was strong enough to remove tattoos.

"And . . . what about the man in the paintings?" I said. I was determined to bring this to a head.

"What about him? Claire said she didn't think he was real," said my mom.

"But *you* do."

"Of course I do," she said. "And so do you. I think it's a wonderful way to remember him."

But I *couldn't* leave it at that. I *had* to know which picture of my dad was the real one: the man who shared his wisdom with me when I was a little kid, the hero swooping me up on

172

golden wings, the big man strutting through the grass on giant legs, the guard in the garden wall, the slacker in the field, the thinker on the breast-shaped rock, the angel cast in stone?

Or the man who—if Claire's grandmother was right—was cheating on my mother. Which was he?

I asked her.

"What difference would it make now?" she said. "What would be gained?"

"I need to know, Mom. That's what would be gained," I said.

She looked me in the eye and seemed to make a decision: "All right," she said. She breathed a long sigh. I sat across from her, my arms still folded.

Looking down at the tabletop the whole time as if she was reading the story from the grain in the wood, she told me how she and Dad had been nearly out-of-control happy when they first moved into the caretaker's cottage. Before long, I was born and their happiness increased all the more, a couple of years slipping by in this blissful state.

Then, on one warm day in April, when I was about three, a van pulled up to the Big House and from the car following it, stepped a woman holding a little girl by the hand. From that day on, it all changed—at least for my mother.

Mom said she could see from the first how Claire's mother looked over the place like she owned it. Dad jokingly told Mom he now had *three* bosses: Mom, Claire's grandmother, and now Claire's mother.

Mom wasn't laughing.

Then Dad started spending more time up at the Big House.

Claire's grandmother had been worried about keeping everything as it *was,* but Claire's mother wanted all kinds of changes—a studio fixed up, a room for her child, the kitchen remodeled—and Dad suddenly wasn't around as much as he had been, and sometimes came back very late, sometimes with booze on his breath. ("She said I should have a drink when I was done building the counter. Seemed like it would be rude to turn her down.")

Then he and Mom started having arguments about little things: who left the lid loose on the pickle jar, whether wooden spoons should be washed in soap or not, how he left his shoes in the middle of the floor—like that.

"I saw where things were going," my mom said, "or at least I thought I did, and finally one evening—your father wasn't home yet. He said he was trying to get some work finished so I was holding dinner. There was a banging at the door. You were doing homework in the bedroom and I answered right away so you wouldn't be disturbed.

"It was Evelyn, Claire's grandmother. She was red in the face. 'I found your husband and my daughter—together, out in the garden,' she said. She raved on about how she wasn't going to have her daughter disgraced by some handyman—this from someone who had been hired help herself," my mother added. "Then she told me, 'I want you all out of here.' "

" 'Together?' What do you mean?" my mother had asked.

" 'You and I are both adults,' she said. 'You know what I mean.' And she said she was calling a truck first thing in the morning, and we were to leave the cottage the next day, or she'd have us evicted. I think if it wasn't so late, she would have kicked us out right then.

"He—your father—came back a short time later with his shirt buttoned all wrong and red on his cheek, and I told him this was it, it was her or me. He said he didn't know what I was talking about and swore nothing was going on, but I told him what old Mrs. Harding had said.

"He tried to explain that he was posing for a painting. He hadn't told me, thinking I wouldn't understand. And I didn't, especially hearing about it like I did. I wouldn't listen. I said I didn't want to hear it and I said how Evelyn wanted us to leave, that I was taking you and getting out of there and that he could come with me or not, but I wasn't going to stay there and share him with someone else. He got a very sad look in his eyes and said OK.

"I wanted to get away from there as fast as possible, and we found this place right away—I'd seen the For Rent sign before—and your dad found work with a landscape company.

"And that was it?" I said. "You never believed him about what he was really doing?"

She looked at me with the kind of look people give you when they really feel sorry that you've said something stupid and they're trying to figure out how to not make you feel so bad.

"Marriages are not always perfect," she said. "We had problems before, when we were starting out."

I didn't say anything. I wanted to hear what they were, but I guess I was afraid to ask. She went on anyway.

"I was much younger," she said. "I was jealous of the time he spent doing things for others. It was kind of like a weak spot he had, I used to think. When somebody asked, he went."

"Mom," I said, relieved it wasn't anything worse, "I thought you told me once that's what you *liked* about him?"

"At first," she said, "but then I think it grated on me. I mean where were we in all that generosity? And there were other things."

She seemed to hesitate a second, like the way you do before going off the sixteen-foot dive. Then she took a breath and jumped. "He lost at least one of his jobs when he got caught in the house with one of the women there. That was before we were married, but we had been going out for a while."

I couldn't say anything. My dad?

"But he had a good reason this time," I said. "The paintings. Why didn't you believe him?"

"I was younger, like I said," she said. "And I assumed things. I never thought that red on a cheek might be paint, or a rumpled shirt might be from posing. Maybe I should have seen . . . maybe I *shouldn't* have jumped so quickly to conclusions."

Her eyes were filling with tears. "And then tonight when I saw them . . ."

"You never *saw* the paintings before?" I said before it hit me:

Of course she hadn't. Claire's mother had hidden them and then we left.

She shook her head, and tried to blot the tears with the back of her hand, wiping it on her robe. She had her other hand flat on the table and I put mine, already bigger, over it.

"I guess what you're asking . . . in some way, he was *all* of those things in the paintings. I knew the way he cared for you—like the one with the golden wings. But some of them I didn't know much about—like the dreamer side of him, and I guess this bothered me, too, that somebody else was finding out things about him I didn't know."

She was quiet for a while. "In the end . . ." she said in a small voice, "I saw he *wasn't* perfect, but he *was* a good man." She looked right at me. "It was only a few months we were here when he died. You weren't even eleven yet. How could I tell you?" She looked down into her murky tea. "I never *would* hear him out—I was just too hurt. I didn't know. I just *didn't* know."

She turned her hand over and gave mine a squeeze.

"What *could* you really know, Mom?" I said. "You were only doing what you thought best."

And when it comes down to it, what else *can* anyone do?

I went to her side of the table and hugged her still sitting there. Her head felt warm against my chest.

21

TWENTY-ONE

And as for the big idea I hatched at the festival?

The next time Claire and her mother had me over for dinner I dropped it on them. We sat in the rundown dining room in the Big House. On the walls all around us were hung, one above the other, all the way up to the ceiling, dozens of Claire's mother's paintings.

"She can't even fit them all in here," said Claire as I stood back to squint up at the very highest. "So every once in a while she takes some down and puts others up. You saw the others laying all around the house like old furniture?"

While her mother worked in her studio, Claire and I put the meal together. Once again, nothing fancy—a big, over-brimming pot of vegetables and beans served out on a pile of noodles with a loaf of black bread in the middle of the table as big as my head, which we ripped off pieces from as we ate (the bread, that is). And here, waiting for the right time, just as we were buttering the last pieces of bread, I hit them with the details of my Super-Sure-Thing, Guaranteed-Can't-Miss Big Idea.

"You're still thinking about selling the place, I guess?" I opened.

Claire quickly glanced at her mother.

"If it comes to it," her mom said. "I haven't given up on the idea. Things are tight, and I'm sure Claire told you it's all or nothing."

"Well, I have a plan," I said, "that will let you keep it."

They waited, looking at me.

"Give it away," I said.

"What?" they said together.

"Not all of it," I quickly added. "Only as much as you don't need." I paused to let this sink in, then went on: "You can't keep it *all* up, like you said. And you can't sell *any* of it off without losing it all. But no one said anything about *giving* some of it away."

"To whom?" said Claire's mother, looking at me like she couldn't be sure if I was *on* something or *onto* something.

"To everyone—for a park," I said.

Claire's mother didn't say anything. Maybe I wasn't making sense, like one of those wild kids raised by groundhogs or something and no one can understand what they're saying? Gruunt, gruunt.

"How would this help?" said Claire, with some small

hope in her voice for Wild Boy slurping up their noodles. “What would we gain from it?”

“A tax write-off for ever and ever,” I said. “First of all, it would be a gift—for charity—and you could pay less income tax. Number B: You’ll have less property, and so you’ll have less to keep up and less property tax, and roman numeral III, with the right deal, you might even get them to cut down whatever tax you had left.”

Even though I didn’t understand *all* of that paper Emily made me read, some of her other sexy talk about mortgages and tax breaks must’ve rubbed off.

“Do you think they would take it?” Claire said.

“I don’t know for sure,” I said, “but remember I told you about the landscape guy at the film festival? He was interested in knowing more about the property. He said he worked with the Parks Board. Here, he gave me his card.”

I gave it to Claire, who looked at it and gave it to her mother.

“But the house itself costs a lot just to keep going,” said her mother, taking a bite of bread from the big chunk in her hand.

This, I knew, would be the touchiest part of the plan. I took a breath and dived in. “Also after the movie,” I said, “at least three or four people gave me their phone numbers and asked about buying your paintings,” I said to her mother.

“My paintings?” Claire’s mother stopped chewing.

Claire and I were quiet for a moment, waiting for some

speech about how she would *never* part with them and how I was an ignorant knucklehead for even *suggesting* such a thing.

Claire suddenly spoke. "Mom, remember you told me that once a painting is done, you move on past it; you forget about it? Besides"—she looked up at the walls around her—"we're running out of room."

Claire's mom thought again for a long time, rubbing her nose with the back of her hand, which had a blue paint stain on it.

"It's a good plan," she finally said, "but I don't know. Maybe it *is* time we moved on."

She looked out the dining room window, which framed a large weeping willow hanging over the log bridge that crossed Snake Creek.

"It is a good plan, though," she repeated.

We finished the meal in silence but I felt I'd made my point. As my dad said, "It's better to give and forget."

So in the end, they went along with letting me test the waters, anyway, giving the guy a copy of "Memory Mansion," for starts. Whatever came of it would come of it. Whatever they would decide, they would decide. There's no predicting people. Some like burnt cookies.

There was one major loose end still hanging from my unraveled summer so one day when I saw there was no YAC meeting, I went over to Emily's house after school.

"Neal!" she said, when she answered the door. "What are

181

you doing here?" She looked around nervously like I'd brought a SWAT team with me.

"You put me off on the phone, and ignore my notes," I said. "So I thought I'd come see you in person."

"What about?"

"Well, first of all about putting me off on the phone and ignoring my notes. I must've left a dozen in your locker."

"I told you I was busy with school starting and everything." I noticed she wasn't inviting me in.

I didn't know how to tell her I wasn't buying it. We both stood there staring at each other for a moment.

"I saw your movie," she said, finally breaking the silence. "Part of it anyway."

Bhandaru, always the showman, ran festival films on monitors in the lunchroom for a week or so after the big event.

It suddenly hit me that she had seen *Claire* in the movie and put one and one together. Accounting was her strong point after all.

"So you like this film thing?" she said.

"Yes," I said. "Like I told you, I think I'm starting to get interested in it."

"Oh," she said.

"I finally found something to do, like you said I should. It's fun."

"Lots of things are fun, Neal, but there has to be more to it," she said.

"You make it sound like 'fun' is bad," I said.

"I didn't say—" she started to say.

"It's not what you didn't say," I cut her off. "It's how you didn't say it." I thought I'd get a laugh out of her.

Not even a smile.

"Neal, you're making less and less sense," she said, taking a quick glance back into the house. I thought maybe her mom or dad had come home early from work.

"To you, I guess," I said.

If I had some idea this was going to lead to an understanding with Emily, it was the wrong idea.

"Look, Neal," she said. "I think big dreams are fine. And I'm happy you finished something you started, but there's a big difference between making a movie for some high school thing and the real thing."

"I know," I said. "But it's a start, and maybe I could use the tape—"

"Em!" Somebody—a guy—was calling her from inside the house. It wasn't her father.

"I'll be right *there,*" she called back.

"Who's that?" I said.

"Just somebody from the club," she said. "We're working on a project."

"That guy I saw you with at school?" I said. I thought of the guy who had come to tell her that the meeting was moved.

"Look, Neal," she said, ignoring my question. "I don't want to get in your way."

It was like we were in two separate cars, coming to where

the highway split, and I could see she was going the other way, but suddenly her eyes got like tinted windows—I couldn't see in.

"You're *not* getting in my—" I started to say.

"Neal." She touched her fingers to my lips. "I thought of calling you lots of times in the last couple of weeks, but it's like I just don't know what to say to you anymore."

Her fingers were cool. I started to talk again, but she pressed slightly.

"I haven't felt good about this," she said. Her eyes were getting wet. "Don't you see? You have something you think you want to do and I wish I could be there for you, but I can't. I just can't. I thought you would understand."

"Em!" Calling her again.

"Look, I have to go," she said, kissing me a peck on the lips and going inside and gently closing the door.

And the funny thing was, as I turned and started walking down the path away from her front door, I was quiet; thinking. But in a block or so, I found myself whistling.

When I saw Claire again later that week, I told her I gave the tape to the landscape guy and that I didn't know when I'd hear anything.

"That's fine," she said. "Mom needs time to get used to the idea, anyway."

Claire and I were sitting on the flat-tired wagon out in the Sea of Tranquillity. It was getting dark a little earlier now and the weather was cooler. I had my arm around her.

"Whatever comes of your movie otherwise," she said, "people really liked it."

"I guess I was surprised," I said.

"That they liked it?" she said. "What's not to like?"

"No, I mean how much the whole thing of *showing* it got to me."

I told her that as my movie played across the screen in the darkened auditorium, I looked around at all these other people—most who I didn't know—staring ahead, their faces all lit up. I began to see that the images they were watching weren't just *mine* anymore, but were part of some larger thing.

"What thing?" said Claire, snuggling in to me.

"Well," I said, "it's like they're *everybody*'s. Now that they're out there, *everyone* can hold them in their memories for me. I can let them go."

"Like Mom with her paintings," said Claire.

"Right," I said. "And I don't have to worry about losing them anymore. I mean, it's not like *everybody's* going to forget."

"Mmmm," said Claire. "Sounds like your plan for here, too. Give it to everyone and get to keep it."

"Exactly," I said. "And if I want to do this—give away my memories—I *also* have to get out of my own selfish way of thinking about them."

Something suddenly occurred to me. "You know," I said, "I think I finally figured out who Bhandaru meant back when he was talking about the 'ghost in the viewfinder.' "

"Who?" she said. "Your dad?"

"No, when I got all broken up from your mom's paintings, for a little while there all I could see was my own eyeball reflected back at me. He was talking about *me*."

"Neal," said Claire.

"What?" I said.

"Be quiet."

And in the small tent of my coat, out there in the cool of the late-summer-night field, we held each other and kissed. I had that strange and wonderful feeling again of flowing out of myself and I had the sense at last to keep my mouth shut.

At least for words.

But talking with Claire like this has got me thinking.

Bhandaru did say something once about how you could study movies—*film*—in college. I could get some more information about it from him—what schools and the costs and everything. My grades weren't so hot, but the movie would probably count some in my favor. And more than just something to study in college, film might be my ticket out of my small, sad world of old memories to a place where I can connect with what's going on around me, right here, where I am; right now, in the present, and—Yes, here it is:

Get on with my life!

If I truly wanted to make films that made sense to other people, like I told Claire, I'd have to get *out* of my own selfish way of thinking. I'd have to believe that I'm not the only one that the world is dumping on, that other people have bad things happen to them and get sad and mad and frustrated.

("And good things, too," Claire reminded me.)

I'd have to truly open myself to how other people felt. And I'd have to truly show my *own* feelings, like Bhandaru said: I would have to be *generous* with my images. Wear my heart on my sleeve.

So maybe making films would be my bridge—the connection I was looking for and didn't even know it—to the bigger world of real people; the connection I wasn't finding as a bagboy or a busboy or a paperboy or a stockboy.

And maybe these images that I had been keeping to myself all these years—that I felt funny talking about? That I was even a little afraid of? (Was I losing my mind?) Instead of just running them as *private* movies in my head, scratching the film a little more each time, wearing it a little thinner, now I could be *sure* I wouldn't lose them since they would always be out there somewhere.

It *is* better to give.

Meanwhile, by the way, here was my *own* life unrolling out in front of me—a blank tape that I could use to fill up with my *own* images of my *own* self out in the Wide World.

And as for "the next logical thing," that my father always warned I might get sucked into before I knew what hit me?

How's this for logic?

I get Claire nearly killed and her favorite horse put down and yet Claire and I wind up together.

Except for my blundering apology way back in the diner, there's been absolutely no mention of this disaster. I see this, by the way, as a case of *Claire* giving and forgetting: giving

187

me a future by forgetting the one thing that could have stopped it dead.

I know she's done this completely in the way you know these things. How, when we're sitting high up on the wagon seat, tipping off into space, there's none of the distractions I felt with Emily. Claire is totally *there* for me.

But I've also been thinking I didn't really understand what Dad was trying to get across to me. I'm thinking what he was actually saying is that it's a mistake to try to separate out work and love and life and line them up in pieces like that. That in life, what is "logical" for one person may not make any sense for another. That you don't always *go* from A to B to C. When I look at the way he actually worked and loved and lived, it was like they were all together in one big chunk.

I'm not saying I've got it all figured out, but if I get the work and love part down, I have a strong feeling that the life will follow.

Like Jake at his counter at the height of the rush, spinning in his dance of scrambled eggs and toast, like when I'm with Claire and I don't have to fight to be understood, like when I'm looking up on a screen at what I've shot and know I'm reaching people: not sitting aside and worrying about things, but lost in them. Wrapped in my own life. That's where I'd like to be.

On the other hand, maybe it will turn out that making movies is good for nothing, and I'll stay as useless as some people seem to think I am.

Like my dad once told me about Osage oranges:

881

"It's important to have some things that aren't used for anything."

And I'll sketch myself in beside all the other useless things that I've drawn in my book: overlapping ferns blurring a hill-side, the grays and pinks of a fungus growing in rings on a dead stump, fog laying like a dropcloth on low ground in the morning, water that pools gray in ice-rimmed ponds in winter and flows slow and green in summer, its surfaces all itchy with life, a sky-blocking tree as big around as I'm tall and reaching into the roof of leaves overhead where it and all the others finally merge in that mutual sky.

Yes, maybe I'll be as useless as all of this some day.

And maybe that wouldn't be all so bad.